BOHEMIA BELLS

by

Lucy Lakestone

VELVET PETAL PRESS

Florida

Published by Velvet Petal Press, Florida

Learn more about the author at LucyLakestone.com

Cover design by Sky Diary Productions

Original photo by AllaSerebrina, DepositPhotos

Kindle ISBN: 9781943134151

Print ISBN: 9781943134168

First edition

PART 1

*B*eing stuck in a cold freezer with a hot guy seems like the perfect romantic setup. I can see the sizzling scene now, the way it would unfold on a TV show. In fact, I probably *have* seen it. He's handsome and considerate. He wraps his arms around you as your situation becomes more dire. He suggests body heat would be the best way to keep warm. And given the sparks you generate together, you're totally in agreement.

Only here we were, Bennett and I, stuck in a walk-in freezer with a light bulb as our only heat source. The situation was more desperate than dreamy. And the tune leaking through the door from the caterer's kitchen just seemed to taunt us: "I've Got My Love To Keep Me Warm."

Maybe Bennett had ocean-blue eyes, sun-streaked brown hair, an adorably scruffy beard and an impish grin, but I was having none of it.

"Millie. Calm down. We'll make it in time." Bennett

flashed me a "please don't be mad" version of that intoxicating smile. "You don't really blame me for this, do you?"

"First, I cannot be calm, and my rage is the only thing keeping me from freezing right now. Two, I don't see how we can be on time — "

"If not, at least we know they'll find our bodies when they come back for *that.*" He nodded at the elephant in the room. Actually, an elephant would have been preferable. It was a hideous ice sculpture of a mermaid and a merman engaged in a kiss. Worse, both of them had nipples like arrowheads. Bright, pointy nipples. Even the ice couple looked like they were cold.

I rubbed my arms, because it was Florida and a warm December — outside, at least — and I hadn't dressed for the Arctic. The sweater was insufficient. And my phone, which might have offered a way out, was locked in my car.

I looked up at the gleaming breasts of the ice monstrosity. "Even if we get out of here before they come back for *that,* it will be too late for you to finish your sculpture. I might be able to put out any other wedding fires that come up, but this thing that you have fought for and promised will be a pile of sand in the middle of the ballroom."

"Have faith. I'm halfway done."

I glowered at him. "It looked like a pile of promising lumps yesterday afternoon."

"See! Promising!" Bennett moved closer and put an arm around me.

I shrugged him off. "Don't touch me!"

He put his arm around me again and whispered in my ear. "That's not what you said two nights ago."

OK, so, yeah, there's some backstory here.

It started one night four months before, when the Zora gallery held its opening in downtown Bohemia, across the lagoon from Bohemia Beach. My friend Thea's cool pop-up paper sculpture was on display, along with the video she did with a bunch of people I knew from the arts scene. I'd helped the stars of the video with their costumes and had gotten to know several of their circle at the art school and theater over the past year.

I'd wangled the night off from waitressing at the Double Diamond Diner — oddly, my only job at the moment. Usually I juggled more than one while I tried to figure out what I wanted to do with my life. I'd worked at the library and the Chamberlain Theater, among other places, trying to determine where my talents would fit best. I knew I was creative. After photography, painting and sculpting classes and a stint in the costume shop, I just didn't know where to invest that artistic energy.

All I knew was that there was no way I was going into the family business. If I never stepped foot in Romano Funeral Home again, it would be too soon, much to my parents' dismay.

That night of the gallery opening, everyone was buzzing with the news that Alex and Sloane had gotten engaged, and I walked up to them to offer my congratulations.

"You're going to be a beautiful couple," I said to Sloane. A potter who studied at the Bohemia School of Art and Design, she had long, reddish-brown hair and almost always wore a cute little dress, at least outside of the pottery studio. Alex was a blond Adonis type. There was always a charge between them, and as he took her arm and leaned in and kissed her neck, I wondered what it would be like to feel that with someone. I mean, I'd *been* with a guy, a short-term boyfriend I'd rather forget, but I'd never really had strong feelings for one. I was usually too busy to date anybody anyway, and the guys who came on to me while I was waitressing tended to be more drunk than charming.

"Oh, Millie, I'm so happy," Sloane said, clasping Alex's hand as he beamed.

"So am I," he said to her, then to me: "I hear you did an awesome job organizing the costumes for *Midsummer at Midnight.*"

"I was just an assistant," I said. "But they did let me create our part of the show bible. That was really fun, pulling together all the themes and fabrics and looks that Penelope designed."

"I saw it. It was fantastic," Alex said.

"You saw it?" I swallowed. "Um, how?"

"I had a VIP tour backstage with a few other donors, and Penelope showed it to me."

That explained a lot. Alex served on the art museum board and was plugged in to several local arts organizations. Somehow he found time to write, too, and I'd heard he was about to publish his first novel.

"You're one of those incredibly efficient people, aren't you?" Sloane looked at me closely. "I mean, whenever we go to the Diamond, it's like you're on wheels, you're so fast."

"Ha! I've never been good on roller skates."

She chuckled. "What I mean is, Penelope says you're super-organized, and your job at the theater has ended, right?"

"Yes," I said, wondering what she was getting at. "It ended when *Midsummer at Midnight* closed. I'm picking up some extra shifts at the diner while I figure out what to do next."

"I know what you're going to do next. You're going to plan my wedding."

"What?" My mouth dropped open.

"We'll pay. Generously," Alex said. I had no doubt about that. The guy was loaded.

"But why me? I've never planned a wedding before."

"Because you'll be awesome at it," Sloane said. "Cali talked about your great eye in her photo class."

"She did?"

"Yes, and I saw your work at her gallery," she said. "You have a sense of beauty and a knack for organization. And you're our friend."

"That's all?" I guess my skepticism was evident.

"That's *huge*," Alex said. "Also, all the other wedding planners in town are either booked or don't want to deal with a Christmas wedding."

"Ah-ha!" I said.

Sloane laughed. "But seriously, you'll be great, and I'd rather deal with someone I know. I don't want it to be insanely extravagant —"

"I told her to be as extravagant as she likes," Alex said. "Especially when it comes to her lingerie."

"Alex!" Sloane smacked his arm and turned ever so slightly red.

He grinned. "I need more wine. You two talk it over." He headed to the refreshments table.

"I'll let you handle your own lingerie," I said.

"Uh, yeah, I have plans for that already," Sloane said *sotto voce*. "I know this is kind of a cliche, but moving to Bohemia Beach changed my life, so I want a beach theme. If we can get Trifles over on the boardwalk, that would be perfect. Cali's going to shoot the photos, so that's taken care of. I'm hoping Ez can talk her band into performing. Alex has an idea about the caterer, someone he wants to sponsor the museum's next gala, so he's trying to curry a little favor by hiring them. He's good at that." I nodded, trying to keep up. "I'm going to ask Thea to create the invitations. Penelope's going to make my dress. We're not going to have conventional bridesmaids, since most of my friends are working the wedding, and I didn't want to leave anyone out. So really, you just have to wrangle decor, the venue, the caterer, a really good bar, and whatever fantastic thematic elements you want to bring in."

"Um, OK. I think I can handle that." *That's all, huh?* My head was spinning, but my hyper-organized brain was already taking mental notes.

"Give it some thought, and we'll meet this week to get into specifics. We'd love to do it Christmas Eve."

Christmas Eve, when everything and everybody cost triple. But Alex and Sloane didn't seem to mind, and I started making phone calls right away. By the time we had our first meeting, I'd already booked Trifles' ballroom with a deposit from Alex, who said he had the caterer lined up and would introduce me.

With my head full of details, and with a nice deposit of my own in the bank, I was ready to apply the creative half of my brain toward coming up with something outstandingly beachy to set their wedding apart.

I'd searched the web, burned my retinas viewing Pinterest and its endless crafty images, interviewed friends and bought a handful of bridal magazines. The suggestions I got ranged from a Yacht Rock theme to bringing in a fishbowl for every table. One thing I knew for sure was that I didn't want anything to do with small living creatures that might not survive the evening. That went for doves and butterflies, too.

One of my fellow servers at the diner, Phil, suggested bridal beach volleyball, but he lost interest when I reminded him that even in central Florida, December wasn't usually bikini weather. The florist was all set with gorgeous shell-enhanced bouquet designs, trimmed with crystals in Christmas colors. The hall had a stunning view of the beach already. But nothing struck me as the right kind of show-stopper until I was watching the Travel Channel late one night in early October and I saw Bennett Westyn.

When I tuned in, he was in the middle of an interview, so I didn't know his name yet. He was dusted with sand, in the heart of a giant arena in Japan, where sand sculptors from all over the world were plying their talents to create massive works of art. The theme of the exhibition was "Mythology," and he'd created a dragon curled around a brood of hatching eggs, with baby dragons opening their mouths and stretching their wings, delineated in stunning detail. The mama dragon's scaled neck arched, with open air beneath it. It seemed completely impossible that it was just sand.

"It's only sand and water. Everybody asks that," Bennett told the camera, his blue eyes mesmerizing. "You just have to pack it really well and take care when you're carving. This stuff is creamy. Beautiful sand."

I'd never thought of sand as beautiful before. I liked walking on the beach as well as anyone, but I'd never seen sand as a source of art. I'd seen sand castles, of course, but nothing like this. This was amazing stuff. This was the spectacular beachy centerpiece I needed for the wedding.

I wasn't sure who I'd get to carve this magical artwork, just two months later on Christmas Eve, but my mind was made up. I needed a sand sculptor. As the show went through all the sculptors' work with interviews and flashbacks, I wondered if any of them would suit. They seemed to be from everywhere — Canada, Italy, Russia, the Netherlands. I didn't think even Alex would spring for airfare for a sand artist from that far away.

Besides, I didn't want to get Alex involved. I wanted to surprise the couple. I knew surprises were dangerous, but Sloane had told me she didn't want to know all the details. She wanted to be enchanted like all her guests when she walked into the hall. And I so loved the idea of being the architect of this oceanic wonderland, I didn't say no.

Bennett's face flashed on the screen again, and this

time, his name was displayed. And under his name, it said he was from — Bohemia Beach!

A Bo Beach boy? That seemed too fortuitous for words. How come I'd never heard of him? Then again, I'd never heard of anyone in Bohemia showcasing sand sculptors. Otherwise, I thought wryly, I'd probably have tried sand sculpting, too.

At that moment, I looked up his website and sent him an email, asking if we could meet as soon as possible about a sand sculpting job. I didn't get specific, just said I was an event planner and that I wanted him for a gig in December in Bohemia Beach.

I wasn't sure how an international sand star would feel about working a wedding on Christmas Eve, even if it was in his hometown. My best shot, I thought, was to convince him in person.

BENNETT COULDN'T MEET me until a Saturday night in mid-November, far too close to the wedding for me not to worry. I had almost six weeks, but still. If he said no, I'd have to come up with a Plan B pretty fast. And I refused to come up with a Plan B. Maybe it was because I liked to think positive. Or maybe it was because I couldn't stop thinking about Bennett's blue eyes.

No, that couldn't be it. I was immune to eyes.

I knew this because Phil, my fellow waiter, had dazzling green eyes and had been unable to persuade me to go out with him on numerous occasions. Of course, Phil was kind of dopey, and I once saw him eat fifty pancakes on a bet. It wasn't pretty.

Tonight, he wasn't helpful at all. He spent most of his time at a booth flirting with a trio of young women wearing department store nametags and excessive eye makeup. I nudged him with an elbow as I jogged by with two burger platters, three gyro plates and a stack of onion rings, but he just gave me a dirty look and kept right on chatting. Normally I wouldn't mind, but I had to get out of here right at eight-thirty if I was going to meet Bennett at nine as promised. Petros, the Double Diamond's gruff but lovable owner, wouldn't let any of us leave if there were unhappy customers.

The diner was slammed for dinner with early Christmas shoppers and a clientele made all the more frisky by the first real cold front. The weather was perfect: 70 degrees, light breeze, sunny. November in Florida. Summer was hell, hurricanes were a pain in the ass, but Novembers were why we lived here, or moved here, or stayed. Sometimes we convinced ourselves that it was because of the beach or the palm trees, but for me, it was November. And most of December.

I harbored no romantic notions of a white Christmas. When you can take a walk on the beach on Christmas Day without even thinking about a coat, with the sun sparkling on the waves and the promise of a holiday dinner outside on the patio, you don't think about snow at all. The soft sand between your toes does just as nicely.

This was the kind of thing I had rattling around in my head as I waited tables: thoughts on the season or my latest artistic project or overheard conversations. Multiple streams of thought helped me work faster, the way listening to music can help you get things done. Speaking of which, the diner had a great collection of classic holiday tunes. As I worked, I hummed along to Bing Crosby and the Andrews Sisters singing "Mele Kalikimaka," a dash of Hawaiian holiday joy.

The music added to the cheer of the tinsel garlands and sparkly snowflakes dangling from the ceiling. Lush red poinsettias glowed in the sills in the big windows at each booth, flanked by gaudy angel figurines. Even the jingle of the bells on the door added to the festive feeling, and for a moment I almost forgot the stress of planning the wedding and my need to impress Bennett Westyn.

Another jingle at the door drew my gaze as I delivered a couple of dinners to one of the booths. My eyes popped as I realized who it was: Bennett Westyn in the flesh. But our meeting wasn't for another hour!

Then I remembered I'd never told him where I worked. This was happenstance. He'd insisted on meeting me at night, so I'd suggested The Junction Box, my friends' favorite hangout by the tracks. Apparently, he was grabbing dinner first.

I made it to the hostess station in an instant.

"I'll take this gentleman," I told Stacy. "Booth Four."

"But it's just him. He could sit at the counter," she whispered to me behind a menu.

"No one is waiting," I whispered back. And, my lifted eyebrows told her, I wanted to wait on him.

She got the message and handed me the menu with a "Hmph."

I ignored her drama and smiled at Bennett, wondering if I should introduce myself. I didn't think he'd take a waitress as seriously as an event planner. I decided my formal introduction could wait until our scheduled meeting, when I could dedicate myself to convincing him to do the wedding.

He returned my smile, and I almost fainted. TV did *not* do his smile justice. Plus his button-up, sky-blue shirt and jeans did little to camouflage his sinewy sculptor's body.

"Right this way." I led him down the row to his booth. I let him slide in and placed the menu in front of him.

"So, Millie," he said, looking at my nametag, "I'm guessing you're not just a waitress."

I lifted one eyebrow and suppressed a flutter of panic, hoping he hadn't guessed at my little deception. "What do you mean, *just* a waitress?"

"I don't mean any disrespect. But isn't there a chance you were the model for one of these delightful angels?" Bennett nodded at the gilded, Renaissance-style winged ladies in the window holding harps and trumpets, dressed in shiny fabrics, their pouty red lips making them look like holy floozies.

"I don't think I'm tall enough to be an angel," I said drily. More often, people compared me to Betty Boop, with my short dark hair and dimples, brown eyes and less-than-Amazonian height.

"These angels aren't very tall." He grinned and held a hand above one of the foot-high figures.

"I'm not that short, either!"

He laughed. "I'm sorry. I couldn't resist. I'm Bennett." He reached out his hand, and I reluctantly took it. His handshake was firm and dry and warm and — electric. A shock of awareness zipped right through me.

I sucked in a breath, let go and tried to quell the quaver in my voice as I asked, "Do you want something to drink?"

I was surprised to see he seemed as startled as I was. He looked into my eyes and took a moment to respond.

"I — uh — any local beers on tap?" he finally asked.

Two minutes later, I brought him a glass of Bohemia Brewing Company's Raging Reindeer, a seasonal ale.

"Listen, Millie," Bennett said. "Can you pull up a bench and chat for a minute?"

Oh, crap. Maybe he did know who I was, though I'd signed the email with my full name, Milia Romano, so I'd seem more serious. I was named after my Italian grandmother, and she was always serious.

His offer to sit down was tempting, despite his horrible flirting. But Petros would have a fit.

"I really can't," I said. "Busy night."

"When do you get out of here?"

This was getting more and more awkward, and he had no idea why.

I looked up at the wall clock behind the counter. "Um, in an hour, but I have to be somewhere. Do you know what you want?"

Bennett's eyes flicked over my body. If I'd blinked, I would have missed it. Funny. I wasn't offended. I knew my curves were obvious under the retro pink dress of my uniform, and normally I was turned off by that kind of attention. But against all reason, I wanted him to like me, and not just for my brain.

"I have someplace to be, too," he said, "but I can blow it off. I'd rather go out with you."

What the hell? He'd just said he wanted to blow *me* off to go out with *me?* At first, I was amused. Then I was annoyed.

I put on a stiff smile. "I'd hate to get in the way of your date, and besides, I really can't break my appointment."

"Oh, it's not a date," Bennett said. "It's business, actually."

"All the more reason to go."

"In your world, maybe. In mine, I try to do as little work as possible."

"What kind of job do you have?" I asked, wanting to see what he'd say.

"It's not really a job. I have fun, and sometimes I get paid for it."

"So you're a gigolo?" *What am I doing?* Somehow, he'd turned me into a smartass.

Bennett laughed. "Only if *you're* in the market for one."

I felt a bump against my elbow and saw Phil speeding by me with a full tray, shooting me a scowl. I glanced over to the booth with the mall women. They were gone. Now I was the slacker, apparently.

"Can I take your order?"

"For food, you mean?" he teased.

"Uh, yeah. That's what we do here."

"Millie, I bow to your seriousness. I'll take the Beach Bum Burger."

Beach bum. That seemed apt. Funny that this guy implied I wasn't fun enough, while my dad was always telling me how irresponsible I was, even after a couple of years at the local college and an associate's degree in business administration. So what if I needed a few more years to find something I really wanted to do?

"Coming right up," was all I said to Bennett, making my escape to give the ticket to the cooks. We still did things old-school here. I caught my breath by the pass-through window in a cloud of steam from the kitchen, dancing around Phil and the other server as we dropped tickets and picked up plates. Then I was off to attend to my other tables, trying to put the frustrating Bennett Westyn out of my mind for five minutes.

I distracted myself with more orders and thoughts about the wedding favors while lip-synching to Kay Starr singing "The Man With the Bag" on the loudspeakers.

Still, I couldn't keep Bennett off my mind. His casual indifference to the job I was about to offer him grated on me. How could someone make *not* working their goal? For me, work was everything — not just at the diner, but at the theater, in my art classes and beyond. I wanted to learn. To do. To make a mark on the world and, yes, have fun doing it.

If I did hire Bennett for the sculpting job, what kind of job would he do? Would he even show up? There were testimonials on his website. The photos showed outstanding sculptures. Maybe I was just being paranoid. He'd been flirting. That was all.

"Are you sure you don't want to go out with me?" Bennett asked when I delivered his dinner. "If not tonight, maybe later?"

At least he wasn't still insisting on tonight.

"Oh, I have a feeling I'll see you again," I said. "Can I get you anything else?"

He smiled. "If you're not available, then I guess I'll have another beer and a check so I'm ready to rock."

"Sure thing." I returned his smile with more assurance. That and relief. It looked as if he was actually going to meet me later. That is, meet Milia, the wedding planner.

I dropped off his beer and check and asked if everything was good. His mouth was full of burger, so all he could do was nod. (I swear, servers do not plan to ambush you when your mouth is full; it's a matter of synchronicity.)

When I returned to his table not long after, the glass was empty, and he was gone. But he'd left me a pile of cash, including a fat tip — a ten-dollar bill with a phone number scrawled across it in sharp black ink.

At least the ten bucks were a good sign. I could never work with a lousy tipper, no matter how blue his eyes were.

I DID a quick change before I left the diner, doffing my pink uniform dress in favor of black and gray patterned leggings and a dark, tie-dyed tunic top I'd made on a slow night at the theater costume shop — comfy but also a bit dressy. I wanted to come across as a professional. Of course, I wasn't fooling anyone. I was also a professional *waitress*, and he would know that.

But there was nothing wrong with being a waitress. A server. Was there? It seemed like I lived to serve — I was always serving someone else's interests. At least I was getting paid for it, but sometimes, that thought was cold comfort. I wanted to express *myself*. Be the star of my own movie once in a while.

The Junction Box was crazy busy. A typical Saturday night. Ez and the Emeralds were rocking the house. I looked around for Bennett and didn't see him, but I tried not to worry. Then I heard my name.

"Millie! Over here!"

It was Calista Goode — Cali — Sloane's cousin and a great photographer. I'd taken her photo class at the Bohemia School of Art and Design, and we'd become friends. Cali was friends with everyone, it seemed, and she'd introduced me to her crowd, all of which seemed to be at the table. I wandered over.

"How are you? Cute top," said Penelope, chic in one of her pinup dresses, her short blond and pink hair perfectly coiffed.

"Thanks!" I beamed. She was a costume designer, so her compliment was gold. "Where's Jace?"

"He's in New York. He has some meetings about a new show, but I'm neck-deep in the designs for a play in Orlando, so I stayed here. Have a drink."

"I can't, yet. I'm supposed to meet someone."

"Oh? Hot date?" Thea asked with a mischievous twinkle. Her cloud of red curls shone in the fairy lights hung around the bar; The Junction Box had decorated early for Christmas, too.

"Um, no," I said. "Purely professional." Then why did I feel a tingle thinking about the maddening Bennett Westyn?

"It's not for the wedding, is it?" asked Sloane. "I don't want you working on a Saturday night!"

"I work every night," I said with a smile. "And I can't tell you. It's a surprise. You're OK with that, right?"

"I told you, I want to be enchanted like everyone else when I walk into the ballroom," Sloane said. "And all Alex cares about is that you use his caterer." She nodded toward the bar, where Alex was hanging out with the others' boyfriends.

"Actually, he's arranged for me to meet the caterer next week," I said.

"Enough work!" said Penelope. "You must drink!"

I wasn't much of a drinker, but I liked to come here on occasion, get to know my new friends and have one of Neil's cocktails. That reminded me. I needed to go over the bar menu with him; he was handling the wedding drinks.

But I didn't have to do that *right* now. I looked around again. No Bennett.

"OK, just one," I said. "Until my appointment shows up."

I sat at the table as Ez's band broke into a punk version of "Jingle Bell Rock." I told the server to tell Neil to make me whatever his specialty of the night was. I knew by now that trusting him with one's cocktail was always a wise move.

It wasn't long before Neil himself brought me a beautiful, dark drink in a martini glass with a twist of lemon.

"What's that?" I asked.

"A Suburban." He smiled and handed it to me. Condensation glistened on the glass, and the drink gleamed like a jewel in the holiday lights.

"Yeah, but what is it?"

"Try it first," he said mysteriously.

"OK." I closed my eyes and sipped. "Oh!"

"What do you think?" he asked, gray eyes bright, his curling mustache twitching with amusement.

"I think this could get me into serious trouble." Especially since I'd been too busy at the diner to eat. The others chuckled in appreciation. "What's in here?"

"Rye, rum and port. It's a pre-Prohibition cocktail."

"It's aged well," I said.

Neil grinned at my joke. "Enjoy."

"I'll call you this week to set up a chat about the wedding drinks, OK?"

"Looking forward to it." He turned to bride-to-be Sloane and gave her a short little bow, then headed off to the bar.

"I wonder what he looks like under that vest," mused Cali, idly playing with her ponytail.

"I wonder what he looks like under that nineteenth-century mustache," Penelope answered. "Probably pretty cute. I need to talk to him about that."

"Men and their facial hair." I rolled my eyes. "Is the

Santa beard trend over yet?" A couple of sips in, and I was already relaxed. Maybe too relaxed.

"I like the scruff, though. Like that guy." Thea, whose Scottish boyfriend had his own ruddy scruff, nodded toward the door.

Shit! Bennett had just walked in. Yeah, that tight, scruffy beard did do something for his jaw, framing his softly chiseled lips, wreathed in a wry smile as he scanned the room and caught my eye. And walked right toward me.

"Oh-ho, is this your appointment?" Cali asked with glee.

"Please. Don't say anything!" I pleaded as the others perked up.

"Why not?" asked Penelope as Bennett arrived.

"Millie! We meet again!" He scanned the table. "And in such lovely company."

"Hi," I said, trying not to be irritated as he nodded at the other women. There was no way I was jealous. I fumbled in my bag, put some cash on the table and stood. "Can I talk to you for a minute?"

"Aren't you going to introduce us?" Penelope asked loudly.

"No," I said, and the others laughed. "Please?" I asked Bennett.

"You can talk to me all night long," he replied, a teasing note in his voice.

I led him away from the women and toward the corner farthest from the band.

"Please sit." I motioned to the table.

"You first."

"OK."

He sat next to me, not across the table as I would have preferred, and then I realized I still held my drink. "Sorry about this. I don't normally drink on the job."

"You work here, too?"

"No! I mean — I'm sorry." I set my glass down.

Bennett smiled. "Please don't refrain on my account. I intend to be drinking shortly."

"But you're here to meet someone."

"I'd rather be with you," he said, looking around. "Besides, I don't see her. She said she'd be wearing a sparkly Christmas tree pin."

"Oh, yeah." I dug around in my bag, pulled out the brooch and attached it to my shirt.

Bennett's mouth dropped open. "You aren't — "

"Milia Romano. Millie for short. I'm so sorry, but I really didn't have time to talk to you back at the diner, even though I recognized you."

"You are more subversive than I gave you credit for," he said with interest.

"You're not mad?"

"On the contrary. Surprised, yes, but not mad. Curious. So what are you? Waitress? Event planner? International spy?"

"And so much more. Except for the spying."

"And you let me go on and on at the diner," he said, shaking his head.

"I'm sorry. It was just so awkward. I couldn't really talk to you about the job then."

"What kind of job do you want me for, *Milia*?"

"Millie, please." I took a deep sip of my cocktail to quell my nerves. "Sand sculpting, of course."

"Given your little deception, I think we should talk about this on my terms," he said seriously.

Ugh. "OK."

"Over another round of drinks, on me."

"Oh, I shouldn't have another one," I said as the band started one of its rock ballads, an Ez original that always made my heart swell. "One is usually my limit."

"Then we are definitely ordering another one," Bennett said. "Waiter!"

A few minutes later, I had another Suburban, and he had a margarita. His eyes widened when he tasted it. "This isn't like any margarita I've ever had. It's delicious."

"Because they use fresh lime juice instead of crappy mixes, along with really good tequila. If you've lived in Bohemia Beach for long, you know the beach bars don't have anything close."

"Oh, I don't live in Bohemia Beach," he said, taking another sip, his eyes like two wild blue moons over the pale green sea of his drink.

What did he say? "But that TV show — " I sputtered. "I mean, all your bios say you live in Bohemia Beach."

"It sounds good," he said with a shrug. "Sexier than Orlando. It's much cooler if I'm from the beach. Otherwise, you wouldn't have contacted me, right?"

There were other reasons I might not have contacted him, like his cavalier attitude and his apparent facility with lies, but not his geography. "Of course I would have. You're close enough. And your work is really good."

Bennett put down his glass and beamed, then nodded at my cocktail as if to say: *Drink up. We have a bargain.* "I'm so glad you think I'm good, because I am. So what do you need? Seems like late planning for a festival. Is it a fundraiser or something? Or do you work with the zoo?"

"No." I was suddenly reluctant to get to the details.

"Private sculpting, perhaps?" He wiggled his eyebrows.

I sighed and took another sip. *What the hell.* "It's a wedding."

He blinked. Then blinked again. "A wedding?"

"Yes. We can pay your regular fee."

"I don't usually do weddings," he said, the smile gone. "Good God, it's not you getting married, is it?"

"Oh, hell, no," I said, and he laughed. "I mean, I'm nowhere near that point in my life. It's my friend Sloane over there."

"The blonde with the pink and the . . . " He glanced at my chest, and I rolled my eyes.

"No, the one with the long dark hair. Her fiancé is here, too, over by the bar. They're ready to pay, only I'm keeping your appearance a surprise. They want a few surprises."

"Really." The mischievous glint was back in his gaze. "I'm good at surprises."

"Well, I *hate* surprises. I want this to go by the book. The question is, are you willing? It's Christmas Eve. The venue is letting us have the ballroom for two days, so you'll have that long to work on the sculpture. Is that enough time? Do you charge double for the holiday?"

"Do you have double my fee to pay?"

I swallowed. "I have an entertainment budget. Tell me

your fee for Christmas Eve, and I'll tell you if I can meet it."

He closed his eyes for a second, silently mouthing words and numbers. Calculating. He opened them and leaned toward me. Closer. Then closer. His warm breath tickled my skin, and my pulse took off like a rocket. I envisioned his lips touching my neck and frantically waved away the image in my mind as if I was trying to fight off a bee. But then he just whispered in my ear.

The deep purr of his voice would have been ridiculously sexy had he not just rattled off a number that would have paid off my car.

He leaned back and crossed his arms.

"Eight thousand dollars?" I said. "Wow. I'm in the wrong business."

"That's double. You did say double, right?"

"I — yeah."

"That's just double my sculpting fee. The rest is pretty much cost. Wood forms, equipment rental, help for the pound-up, hotel, five tons of sand — "

"Five tons!"

He grinned. "That's nothing, really. And I'd prefer two days to sculpt, not counting the cleanup, which I'd like to do after the holiday. So I'd need to get in a day earlier so we can do the pound-up."

"Pound-up?" I asked weakly. This all sounded more complicated than I thought. Not to mention expensive.

"We have to set up a sandbox to protect the floor, bring in the sand, wet it, compact it in the wooden forms, add additional levels, add more sand, compact it. It's a lot of work, and it can be loud. So you might want to check with the venue to make sure noise is OK."

The biggest sticking point would be adding another day, plus the cleanup day. Alex had friends at Trifles on the Boardwalk, but I was sure Trifles would add to his fee. And given it was the holiday season, the ballroom might be booked, anyway.

"I'll have to see if that's possible," I said. "Unless you can pull an all-nighter."

"As much as I like all-nighters," he said, "just the pound-up is exhausting. I have to get some sleep if I'm going to get the sculpture done and done well."

"We'll figure it out. Does this mean you'll do it?"

"If you can meet my needs," Bennett said with a coy smile.

The sculpture would comprise almost the whole entertainment budget, but since Ez said her band's appearance was their gift to the happy couple, I could swing it. I just hoped I wouldn't have buyer's remorse.

I smiled. The decision was made, and now I could worry about everything else. "All right. Let's do it."

"We should *definitely* do it," he said, grabbing my outstretched hand and grinning.

Again, I felt that jolt I'd felt at the diner. Pure electricity. His grin faded, and he held on for an extra few seconds, pulling me slightly closer. Closer.

Oh, God . . .

He let go, glowering under a furrowed brow, and took a huge gulp of his drink. "I have a standard contract. Should I send it to your email, Milia?"

"Millie." I took a sip of my drink, too. It only added to the pleasantly terrifying feeling catapulting through my veins, as if I were teetering on a cliff, about to fall into a chasm of unknown depth. "Yes. Thanks. We will pay half up front and half when the project is completed."

"What, you don't trust me?" he asked softly, a playful note in his voice.

"I don't know you."

"We'll remedy that," he said, quirking his lips into a droll smile. "I promise."

"So are you with me, Millie?" Bennett was saying. "Millie?"

"Yes, ass-bolutely," I said, swaying a little at the table. Bennett had pulled his chair even closer, and for the past hour, he'd been sketching with the felt-tip pen he apparently carried around in his back pocket. Fortunately, I carried a sketch pad in my bag for my intermittent artistic impulses, so he hadn't had to resort to cocktail napkins.

I had to admit, Bennett's drawings were beautiful. Of course, with nearly three of Neil's potent cocktails in me, everything he drew looked like it belonged in the Louvre.

He held up the pad so I could get a better look. "You like the idea of the open book with the castle and the prince and princess popping out of it, reaching for each other?"

"It's magical," I said. "Alex is a writer. Sloane is his princess." I sniffled. *Oh, crap.* There might've been a tear in my eye. And Ez and the Emeralds were on a break, so I couldn't blame the music. In the band's place, the speakers were blaring The Kinks doing "Father Christmas."

"Great," Bennett was saying. "Prince and princess. Naked, right?"

"Sure." A tiny light bulb came on in my inebriated brain. Low-wattage, like an LED. "No! *Not* naked!" I added a little too loudly, and a few heads swiveled our way.

Bennett laughed. "You're drunk. This isn't very *professional.*"

"I know. I'm so sorry," I said, taking another sip.

"I like the unprofessional you. Between the frigid waitress and the forbidding wedding planner … "

"I am *not* frigid!" *Shit.* A few more heads turned our way. "See, there you go. Putting me on the defensive. That's a typical man's reaction when any woman isn't interested in him. 'She's frigid.' 'She's a bitch.' Et cetera."

"You're right," Bennett said mildly. "I'm sorry. Poor choice of words."

"Well … " I wasn't sure how to remain outraged in the face of his apology.

"But I'm happy to know you're not frigid."

Argh! He was just starting to win me over, and then he pissed me off again, though his smile showed he was joking.

"Just for the record," I said, "I'd rather be a frigid bitch than a pushover."

"Do you *ever* want to be pushed over?" he teased. Somehow his jeans-clad knee brushed mine through my clingy leggings. He'd been nudging closer with each drink, and his presence was so pleasant, I really hadn't worried about it until now.

"I mean, every girl wants to be pushed over at some point," I admitted. Or the alcohol admitted. "I mean, when the right guy comes along. We want to be swept off our feet, carried off into the sunset, all that crap. Pushed over, but only because we want to be. Sure."

"How's a guy supposed to know when she wants to be pushed over? Will you let me know?"

"We're not going there." An unbidden smile came to my lips, and I tried to twist it into a scowl. But I was pretty sure all I did was show my dimples. "We have to be professionals. We're going to be working together."

"But there's a part of you that wants to be just a little unprofessional, isn't there?" He took my empty glass from my hand and set it down, and then somehow I was holding his hand instead of the glass. Or he was holding mine.

"I will not be seduced the first time I meet you or anyone," I declared, fortunately not loud enough to attract stares this time. But I didn't let go of his hand.

"It's really the second time you've met me. First as a server, and then as a wedding planner."

"And now as a drunk."

"Oh, don't beat yourself up." Bennett wasn't just holding my hand now. He was stroking it. Heat skated across my skin and blossomed between my legs. "It's not like you've never been drunk before," he added.

"Actually, I never get drunk. I usually stop at minor buzz."

His eyes widened. "I'm the first guy to get you drunk?"

"You didn't 'get me drunk,' " I said defensively. "I am completely responsible for my own drunkenness."

Bennett laughed. "OK."

"I need to go home." Before I passed out.

"Can I take you home?"

"Ass-bolutely not. I can walk."

"Are you sure about that?"

"Not really." Damn it, alcohol was like some kind of truth serum. I needed to remember this in the future. If I remembered tonight at all.

"Look, I'll walk you home. Where do you live, anyway?"

"Apartment house. Only a few blocks away. Ez used to live there, and I just moved in after all my roommates moved away."

"Who's Ez?"

"The singer."

"Nice."

"But I'm not in the same apartment. Some guy is in her old apartment, she told me. I'm across the hall. It used to be a hotel, you know, back in the 1920s and '30s."

"Fascinating." Bennett bit his lip.

"Are you laughing at me?"

"Mm-mm," he said, but he didn't open his mouth, just got redder.

"Yes, you are. You are!" I pulled my hand from his and poked him in the stomach.

He barked out something that sounded like a cross between a laugh and an exclamation of pain.

"See, I was right," I said. I looked down. "My glass is empty."

"You were going home, remember?"

"Did I pay? I have to pay Neil. He's a genius."

"Who's Neil?"

"The bartender."

"I said I would pay, remember?" The check mysteriously appeared in Bennett's hand, and he dropped it on the table with some cash. "I'll walk you home."

"But you might try to take disadvantage of me."

He looked like he was trying not to laugh again. "I won't take advantage of you, Millie."

"Oh, thank God."

"That hurts," he said. "I thought you liked me."

"I mean, thank God you're calling me Millie."

He smiled. "Whatever makes you happy. Ready to go?"

"Sure." Not only was alcohol a truth serum, but it was making me more pliant than usual. Was that a good thing?

Bennett touched my elbow lightly, helping guide me to the door, when I felt a presence and looked up.

"You OK? Do you need me to call you a cab?" It was Neil, bow tie and all, looking concerned.

"I'm OK. Bennett is going to walk me home. And that's *all,*" I declared, instantly wondering why I'd needed to say that out loud. Truth serum. Right.

Neil looked Bennett over, then looked back at me.

"He's OK," I said in a stage whisper. "He's a professional."

Neil's gaze snapped back to Bennett. "Professional sand sculptor," Bennett said. "It's really fine. Look, here's my card." He pulled a business card from his phone case and handed it to Neil. "Track me down if you have to. I just want to make sure she gets home safely."

After another moment of inspecting the card and Bennett, Neil seemed to relax. He nodded. "All right. Goodnight. Talk to you soon, Millie."

Neil's hair glinted with red highlights under the Christmas lights as he turned away, and I remembered something.

"Penelope wants to talk to you about your mustache!" I called as Bennett ushered me out the door.

"What was that about? Who is he?" Bennett asked as we walked slowly toward my place amid clusters of late-night partiers. They merrily drifted down the sidewalk like schools of inebriated fish.

"That's Neil, the bartender, er, mixologist."

"Is he your boyfriend?"

"No. I don't have boyfriends."

"Never?"

"There was one for about a month once. Waste of time," I said.

"That's sad."

"Why, you have girlfriends?"

"Um." Bennett, for once, seemed to be at a lack for words. "I've had a couple. Nothing came of them. I don't think relationships are my thing."

"Given your lack of seriousness, that somehow doesn't surprise me." I bumped against him — my, how warm he was — and he steadied me as I tried to avoid a woman struggling with her zigzagging dachshund.

"That's not fair," he was saying as I started walking again. "I can be serious. I'm serious about my work."

"You are not! You told me in the diner you have fun and get paid for it."

Bennett slipped his arm in mine, and I was amazed at how much steadier I felt. "Then you accused me of being a gigolo."

"Well, are you?"

He laughed. "No one pays me. And I certainly don't need to pay them."

"Because you're so cute." I gasped and clapped a hand over my mouth as I realized what I'd said.

Bennett pulled me a little tighter. "You think so? I'm going for handsome, myself, but I guess I'll take cute in a pinch."

"Cute, sexy, whatever." *Oh my God, what the hell?* Trying to be breezy, I kept digging the hole deeper. Damn Neil and his cocktails.

Bennett laughed even louder this time. In fact, he couldn't stop laughing, and his whole body shook against mine, heating me up in the crisp, cool evening.

"I don't know you well sober, but I really like you drunk," he finally sputtered.

I didn't say anything for a minute, afraid of what might come out of my mouth next. "This is my place," I said as we arrived at my pink, art-deco building.

He got me to the front steps and hesitated. "Can I come in?"

"I'm going to be honest with you here, since apparently I can't be anything else when I've been drinking." I shifted my bag on my shoulder and leaned against him. "I'm not entirely sure I can make it up the stairs, so you can help me with that, but then you have to go."

"I can do that," he said, but the disappointment in his eyes almost killed me.

Yes, he had to go. But what I didn't say was that I didn't want him to go, even though the very idea of letting him stay scared the hell out of me.

I keyed in the code for the front door, a new security measure that let us into the tiny lobby, and then he escorted me up the stairs to my place. I unlocked my door and tossed my bag through the opening and deep into the dark apartment, making Bennett chuckle again.

I turned toward him, took a deep breath and tried to sound sober. "I look forward to working with you, Mr. Westyn." I reached out to shake his hand.

"I can't wait to work with you, Ms. Romano, and I anticipate several meetings to make sure we're on track."

"More meetings? You can't just show up and sculpt?" A tickle of panic prickled through me.

"We have to make sure I have the right sand — "

"The venue is on the beach. We can just bring it in."

"No, we can't. We need special sand. Trust me. There's more to discuss."

"We can do it online."

"No, we can't." Bennett grabbed the hand that I'd left sticking out there in midair, and then, in slow motion, he pulled me close. "Personal meetings will be *ass*-bolutely necessary."

I knew he was making a joke. Then why did he look so serious?

He released my hand, but he didn't withdraw. He leaned over me, his hair flopping into his eyes, now all blue sparks and smoke and intensity. Close, so close I felt his breath on my face, he slowly ran a finger along my jaw. All of my senses focused on that one electric touch as my body awakened at his nearness, at his mesmerizing caress. With the swift smoothness of running water, he slid his arms around me and pulled me against his tautly muscled form. Before I could summon a rational thought, his lips found mine.

Sweet. So sweet, with a touch of salt. Margarita and man. Beach? No, that was my imagination, as I closed my eyes and relaxed in his arms and got lost in a sea of sensation as he tasted me.

Heat. He felt me respond, and his sweetness became more complex, more carnal. His mouth moved assertively against mine, deft and warm, sucking on my bottom lip, licking my top lip. Then he tilted his head to consume me, hard and demanding, and I groaned and clutched him and opened to his sweeping tongue.

Too soon, he let me go. I struggled to catch my breath, my eyes wide with shock at my own abandon. I'd been ready to drag him into my place and — and be a pushover.

"I told your friend I'd walk you home." Bennett's voice was rough. "I'll call you soon. Goodnight."

He watched me as, like a robot, I took a few steps backward in slow motion until I was over the threshold. I gingerly closed the door on that tormented, handsome face, not wanting to wake up from this dream.

As addled as I was, under the influence of not just the drinks but that intoxicating kiss, I took a few moments to think about what I really wanted and then looked through the peephole, just in case.

He was gone.

"THANKS FOR MEETING ME HERE." Alex leaned against the railing of Bohemia Beach's short boardwalk, a cool breeze ruffling his dark blond hair in the midday sun. He wore khakis, a button-up white shirt and a tie that flapped in the wind off the ocean. He was about as formal as anyone ever got on an average day in Florida.

Alex had a casual physicality about him, but it was nothing like what I sensed when he was around Sloane. Those two had a kind of crazy chemistry that I'd never experienced. Well, not until recently, anyway.

"I wanted to introduce the caterer to you personally," he said, "partly so he knows he was my particular choice for the wedding. I've been dropping hints about him sponsoring the food for the art museum's next big fundraiser, but I think I need to make him appreciate the opportunity with a nice fat catering job."

"That's pretty cool of him to contribute the food to your event," I said, smoothing my wind-rippled, green satin blouse down over my black dress pants, trying to look as if

I was as organized and efficient as everyone seemed to think I was.

"It's not guaranteed yet. He can be a little prickly. But I'm going to soften him up with lunch at Trifles." Alex pointed down the boardwalk to the large 1920s Mediterranean revival building that housed a formal restaurant and piano lounge, a popular bar, a café and a ballroom. "Did you know I had to pay Trifles extra for the ballroom because they *weren't* doing the food for the wedding?"

"I'm not surprised," I said. "I've done a ton of research on this stuff, and the wedding-industrial complex is one big racket. They charge you double for what they can do and triple for what they can't."

He laughed. "Except you. I might need to raise your fee."

"I'm perfectly content," I said. The truth was, the payoff had been so generous that I'd dropped one of my diner shifts to focus on wedding preps and a new clay sculpture class I was taking at the art school. I just couldn't stay away from those classes.

"They almost killed me for that extra day and the cleanup time, though they didn't have anything scheduled. I can't wait to see what you have planned that you need an extra day to decorate."

"Me either," I said drily.

He laughed again. "I'd decorate the whole ballroom in diamonds if I could, but I have to draw the line somewhere. Thanks for working within my budget."

Barely, I thought, hoping my sand-sculpture plan wouldn't blow up in my face.

Alex straightened. "Here's the caterer now."

The caterer couldn't have looked more different from Alex. In his thirties, I guessed, he wore outrageous billowing chef pants that looked as if a box of crayons had exploded all over them, topped with a red golf shirt accented by a logo. Lime-green Crocs completed the outfit. The man himself sported wiry, dark brown hair trimmed into a tight, Brillo-pad cut, severe sideburns and a tanned face. He was of medium build — not a chef who partook too much of his own creations, I thought — and his lips formed a thin line that bent only slightly upward at Alex's wave.

The wave turned into a manly handshake as the two greeted each other.

"Rafe Broussard, I'd like you to meet Millie Romano, our wedding planner," Alex said. "She has all the details of what we want and will be handling scheduling, tastings, whatever you need. Rafe is the proprietor of Broussard's Catering and Bakery."

"Broussard's Catering and *Patisserie*," the caterer said pointedly.

"Mr. Broussard," I said, sticking out my hand. "It's very nice to meet you."

He took my hand, lifted it and pressed a kiss on to my knuckles. A cold, uncomfortable kiss.

"Call me Rafe, please. It's my pleasure," he said. "I'm always happy to do what I can for Alex."

"I'd like to talk to you about our options," I said to the caterer after I'd reclaimed my hand and resisted the urge to wipe it on my slacks. "We have a fair number of vegetarians and people with, uh, interesting dietary needs on the guest list . . . "

"Not a problem. We have a variety of small plates we can offer that are vegan and gluten-free, as well as specialized entrees, as long as you don't mind the extra fee," Rafe said smoothly as Alex raised his eyebrows with resigned humor. "As for our cocktails . . . "

"Oh, actually, we're bringing in a bartender," I said.

"Really?" He frowned. "But if you want the highest level of excellence — "

"We should be more clear," Alex interrupted. "We're bringing in a *mixologist* from the Bohemia Bartenders."

"Never heard of them," Rafe said with a sniff.

"Neil Rockaway is the director," Alex said. "Owns an excellent bar downtown. Trust me, the drinks will not disappoint."

I took in this new info while silently thanking Alex for shutting down Rafe. Neil owned The Junction Box? I had no idea.

"We'd love for you to do the cake, though," I said.

"As you should," Rafe replied, warming up a tad. "Our cakes are fabulous. We can talk about all the details and taste some samples at our storefront in Bohemia if you like. Bring in your bride," he said to Alex. "And of course you'll want one of my spectacular ice sculptures. They're my signature at any wedding of import."

Wedding of import. I thought I saw Alex bite back a smile as I felt a flutter of panic. "An ice sculpture sounds great!" he said easily.

"Of course, there will be an additional fee." Rafe

smiled, baring rows of tiny teeth reminiscent of the baby corn that no doubt adorned his vegetable trays.

Ugh. I had already engaged Bennett Westyn to produce a spectacular sculpture! Sure, one was sand and one was ice, but wouldn't two be too much?

"Our reservation is for noon," Alex said, walking toward Trifles on the Boardwalk. Rafe fell into step with him, and I trailed the two men, trying not to be blinded by Rafe's pants. "Millie, would you like to join us?" Alex asked over his shoulder.

"Ah, no, I'm actually meeting someone for lunch at the café." And I didn't want Alex to know who, since "who" was the surprise: our sand sculptor, Bennett, to whom I sorely needed to apologize for getting so out of control the other night.

"I've got to run to the men's room," Alex said as we got to the door. "Meet you upstairs?" he asked Rafe.

"Of course." Rafe watched him go inside, then turned to me. "I've never worked with you before," he said pointedly.

"I'm new to the business."

He looked me up and down. "That won't be a problem. I can guide you. I'm a very good teacher."

I tried to ignore the creeps he gave me and forced a smile on my face.

"Milia!" came a voice behind me. *Oh, shit.*

I turned. "Bennett! Just in time. Thanks for meeting me."

"Glad we could do it so soon." His smile dazzled me more than the bright November sun overhead. Behind him, the blue ocean was a faint pretender to the color of his beautiful eyes.

I told myself to get a grip and introduced the men. "Bennett Westyn, I'd like you to meet Rafe Broussard. He's the caterer for the wedding."

"Rafe?" Bennett stopped next to me and looked closely at the chef. Then his eyes grew wide. "Ralph Brucie, is that you? Hell, I wondered what happened to you after you dropped out of the circuit!"

"It's *Rafe,*" the chef snapped.

"So you're a caterer now? Wow. That's fantastic." Bennett's tone was laced with irony.

"And you're still shoveling sand, I presume?" Rafe said.

"All over the world," Bennett said.

"I did some international shows after I left you beach bums, but I grew weary of the travel."

"Oh, yeah, that's right. You were doing ice for a while, weren't you?"

"If you mean winning competitions and making you look like a dirt farmer, yes," Rafe said in a bored tone that seemed to suggest he was anything but calm. And it was clear the tension was catnip to Bennett.

"At least I don't have to worry about frostbite," Bennett said with a smile. "You can see my work on Christmas Eve."

"Why?" Rafe's eyes narrowed. "Are you doing a show here?"

"Show? Hell, no, I'm doing the wedding."

Rafe's dramatic gasp almost made me laugh. "You can*not! I'm* carving an ice sculpture for the wedding."

Bennett turned to me in astonishment. "You hired him after you hired me?"

"I — No. Alex hired him. I didn't know about the ice sculpture. It's — it's his signature," I ended lamely.

"That's right," Rafe said. "It's my signature. And we don't need a sand sculptor bringing dirt into the hall. Unless you're going to be on the beach, in which case we can all ignore you."

This guy was really starting to tick me off.

"Bennett will be in the ballroom," I stated flatly.

"Really?" Rafe's raised eyebrow smacked of artificial drama, but there was no doubt he was peeved. "I'll need to ask Alex about this."

"Don't!" I said. "Please don't tell him. The sand sculpture is a surprise. It's something special and Sloane — the bride — she just loves sand." Well, she loved the beach, but I didn't think she'd mind a little stretch of the truth, given the situation. "Please don't ruin the surprise. I know giving away the secret would upset Alex, too. He wants Sloane to have everything she wants, and she wants them both to be surprised by the decor."

Mentioning Alex's name seemed to reel Rafe in. Alex Alwend knew a lot of people and gave to a lot of causes. He had influence that could make a big difference to a caterer one way or another.

Rafe stood silently for a moment. "I suppose we can work out something as long as my sculpture is far away from his. I don't want any sand near my food, either!"

"Of course not," I said.

Rafe looked at his watch and grimaced. "I have a lunch

to attend. Millie, please call me about our meeting. It was nice to meet you," he said, though his tone suggested otherwise. *Great.* I was going to have to work closely with this stick.

He said nothing to Bennett, only glared at him and stalked into the building.

As the door closed, Bennett burst into laughter.

"You think this is funny?" I asked.

"Probably not, but it's laugh or kill him," he said.

"You worked together?"

"He carved sand, too, once upon a time. We did some competitions and festivals together, that kind of thing, back when I was still doing mostly regional stuff in the U.S. He wasn't very good. Plus he was an ass to work with. Most sculptors are really cool, help each other out, but he treated it more like a sport than an art. He burned one too many bridges and stopped getting calls. He did ice for a while, and then he kind of dropped out of sight. But maybe nobody's heard tell of him because he's calling himself *Rafe Broussard* now."

"He does sound pretty fancy, you have to admit."

"But those shoes."

I glanced at Bennett's feet, clad in worn leather sandals. He wore Army-green cargo shorts and a Tatooine T-shirt. I cocked my head at him while trying not to stare at his legs.

"I'm beach-appropriate," he said.

"Cute T-shirt."

"Sand joke." He smiled. "So are we going up to the swanky piano lounge, or shall we dine formally with Rafe?"

"I'm buying you lunch at the Conch Café downstairs." I led the way to the western end of the building, where a small open-air café, sheltered by a thatched roof, offered an oblique view of the ocean and the parking lot. In warmer months, it would be swarming with beachgoers. Today, there were just a few diners enjoying the weather. Palm trees around the edges of the patio, a tiki or two and bamboo trim gave it an island feel. A slightly surreal steel-drum version of "White Christmas" tinkled from the speakers.

A waitress laden with full plates nodded at us. "Sit wherever you like."

We sat on opposite sides of a small square table. Bennett picked up the laminated menu. "Too early for beer?" he asked.

"I'm not having any," I said. "In fact, I don't know if I'll have anything alcoholic ever again. I wanted to meet you to apologize for my behavior on Saturday. It was totally unprofessional. First, I didn't tell you who I was right away — "

"To be fair, I did try to stand you up so I could take you out," he said.

"That wasn't encouraging," I admitted, and he grinned. "But then I got drunk, and I *never* get drunk, and then — " I couldn't bring myself to say it. I kissed him. Or rather, let him kiss me. Encouraged it. Wanted it. Wanted to kiss every inch of his body and take him to my bed.

Oh, God.

Bennett's smile was gone, and he was looking at me with nothing short of burning intensity.

"Stop that," I said.

"What?" he answered softly.

"Looking at me like that."

"I don't regret a single minute of Saturday night. And I hope you don't, either. To apologize is pointless. We had a moment. I hope we have more."

"Have y'all decided what you want to drink?" The waitress's sudden appearance and high-pitched Southern syllables snapped me out of Bennett's spell, but I still felt hot all over.

"Iced tea? Unsweet?" I asked.

"Sure thing. And you, hon?"

Bennett's face relaxed, and he shot me a tiny smile before looking up at the server and ordering a beer.

"You'll have beer again," he told me when she left. "Or better yet, cocktails."

"Singular. Cocktail. If I ever drink again."

"But you enjoyed it so much. Didn't you?" He wasn't just talking about the drink.

And despite how obnoxious he could be, I did enjoy it. The drinks. Him.

The server brought back a beer, saving me from replying, and we ordered (burger for him; an arugula and chicken salad for me) and spent a few minutes talking about the weather and the venue until our food arrived.

He popped a fry into his mouth and started on his second beer. "How did you get into wedding planning?"

I held up a finger as I finished my first tasty bite. I loved arugula. It actually had flavor, unlike lettuce, which should be banned from all salads.

"Alex and Sloane asked me," I finally said.

"What?" He looked puzzled. "This is your first wedding?"

"As a planner, yeah. I've been a bridesmaid. I've been to weddings. I did some research."

"Wow." Bennett didn't say it, but I knew what he was thinking.

"I know what I'm doing. I'm known for being organized. Ask anybody."

"Chill. I'm fine with it. I got the down payment, and I like you. This will be fun, especially if I get to mess with Ralph."

"He calls himself Rafe," I said. "And you can't mess with him. Too much depends on keeping him happy and productive."

"Ha!" Bennett said. "Ralph has never been happy for five minutes at a time, unless he was conquering somebody else."

"Did he ever conquer you?"

"Hmph. He occasionally beat me in competitions that had a people's choice award, because he made sand castles ninety percent of the time. People love sand castles, so if you try to do real art in a competition like that, you'd better hope there are real judges, too."

"So you hate sand castles?" I asked. "Isn't a castle part of your design for the wedding?"

"It is, but it's only a small part, and I like this design. A prince should give his princess a castle." He smiled. "Besides, I don't think a tasteful nude or an abstract concept piece would go over so well."

I nodded. "I'd like you to be happy with whatever you do."

"I will be," Bennett said. "I don't do anything I don't want to do."

"That's a nice luxury. Most of us can't say that."

"It wasn't always that way," he admitted. "I was apprenticing to be an auto mechanic when I fell into sculpting. I liked working with cars, still do, but it was definitely a job, and a lot of bullshit was attached. I couldn't afford college, and my mom couldn't really help on her admin's salary."

"Your dad wasn't in the picture?"

"He died when I was twelve. Heart attack."

"I'm sorry." I took a sip of tea and pondered what Bennett must have gone through. He made me appreciate my parents and their fixed ideas and impossible standards a little bit more. At least they were still around and wanting the best for me. "Is your mom doing OK?"

"She eventually got promoted, and she just remarried last year. She's doing fine. Moved to Myrtle Beach, where we used to vacation. Golfs a lot. Not really my thing, but I see her occasionally."

"So how did you fall into sand sculpting?"

"Ah. There was a sand sculpting competition at Myrtle Beach during one of our visits when I was nineteen — seven years ago? Shit, hard to believe it's been that long. It wasn't one of the big ones, but some really talented people were there. One of them was Gerald Mercury. He did an interactive thing where he took a few spectators and had them sculpt a quick piece under his direction. I took to it right away, and he appreciated my enthusiasm. Maybe he pitied me a little, too, after learning more about me, but he said he could use a helper. I helped him that weekend, and then I started traveling with him, helping with pound-ups, logistics, whatever he needed. Sometimes I'd help him finish a piece or do the rough sculpt before he came in and did the details. Or I'd do details while he dealt with another piece. And I was always playing with the sand, practicing. We got to one competition up north where a big snowstorm had kept a couple of sculptors from flying in — "

"You can sculpt in the snow?"

Bennett nodded. "I have, but it's not ideal. On this occasion, the build was in an indoor arena. But it was just a weekend event, and there was no time to waste. Gerald suggested to the organizers that I could take one of the empty slots. They were desperate and agreed. It was my first time out, and I won the people's choice award."

"What did you sculpt?"

He looked a little embarrassed. "A sand castle. But it had a dragon, too."

I chuckled. "I saw the dragon you did on that TV special. It was amazing. It's what made me reach out to you."

"Well, that and my stunning good looks, I'm sure." He took another bite of burger, his eyes dancing.

"The Italian guy was better looking," I said, but I couldn't suppress a smile.

"Leonardo? The girls love him. Especially the Italian girls like you."

"How do you know I'm Italian?"

"Milia Romano? Give me a little credit."

I giggled and then covered my mouth. Giggling did not suit a wedding planner at all.

I paid for our lunch and led Bennett around the building to the ballroom. He checked out the loading doors, confirmed a hose was available to water down the sand, and then we went inside.

"I asked them about the noise," I said, "and they said the building was pretty well insulated and it probably wouldn't be a problem, as long as you weren't running the heavy equipment after five. They don't mind a little noise at lunch, but a company has rented out the restaurant for a holiday party on the 22nd in the evening, and they don't want any distractions."

"Not a problem." He walked over to the wall of windows that faced the deck overlooking the beach and looked out. There was an easy grace to his movements that I found mesmerizing. The bright, diffused light brought out the blond streaks in his sandy-brown hair and lit up his face as he smiled at the view. That smile softened the lines of his firm jaw and made those plushly sculpted lips even more inviting. His nose had a subtle bump but almost turned up at the end. His eyebrows had a naturally mischievous arch to them that perfectly complemented those deep blue eyes. Ah, those eyes. They always seemed to have a sparkle that rivaled the ocean's. Boyish charm, that's what it was. I'd never really gone for boyish until now. Not that I was going for him.

I shook myself and tried to pay attention to what he

was saying as he turned toward me and looked around. "Fantastic light in here. Where would you set me up?"

I gestured toward one corner near the windows. "I think here, next to the stage, so you'd get some nice side light on the sculpture, at least while you're working. The truth is, by the time the reception happens, it'll be dark, but people will get a chance to see it before then."

"I have lights. What time is the wedding?"

"It starts at five. Sunset's about five-thirty."

"Ceremony on the beach?"

"Of course," I said. "Unless the weather gods frown upon us. You're lucky you're going to be working inside."

"True, but I've sculpted in the rain more times than I care to admit. Sand can hold up to a lot."

"Why can't you use beach sand?" I looked out at Bohemia Beach, glowing gold in the sun. "It's not pristine white sand here, but it's nice."

"I'll show you." Bennett gestured toward one of the doors that led to the deck and the beach. "Come on."

We left our sandals at the short flight of stairs that led down from the deck, my black strappy ones next to his rough brown leather. I rolled up my pants to my knees, and we walked toward the ocean. A few hardy beachgoers had chairs and towels laid out. No doubt they were escapees from the most northern states who thought 75 degrees was warm enough to swim. Otherwise, the beach was empty.

"I love the beaches here," Bennett said. "Where my mom lives, it's always packed. This is so nice. Puts you in touch with the natural rhythms of the earth when you're not distracted by beach blanket bingo."

"I guess you work on a lot of beaches."

"Fewer than you might think, especially since we rarely use beach sand."

We'd reached the wet sand where the waves were hissing up the beach, edged with glistening white foam. Tiny shorebirds chased them as they retreated. Bennett scooped up a handful of the damp sand and started packing it in his hands. "Look at this." He held out the sand ball. As soon as he set it in my hand, it began to crumble.

"But that's a ball. I can make a sand castle that won't do this."

"Sure," he said, "but you'll be limited in what you can do with it. You'll never be able to make an overhang or an arch, for instance."

"Like your dragon's neck."

"Right! Like in the show." He smiled. "Beach sand wouldn't be as strong, either. Sand from the beach has been tumbled and smoothed over time. The grains are round. They don't want to hang together. When we get sand from the quarry I have in mind, it'll be much more clingy. The grains are angular and stick together. I can make a ball from it and toss it in the air and catch it, and it won't fall apart."

"I look forward to the demonstration," I said. "Do you do a lot of documentaries like the one I saw?"

"Not many. Once in a while I'll get on a news feature with some of the other sculptors, or someone will try a catty reality show, only we get along too well to make it dramatic enough for most producers."

"I didn't see your friend Gerald on that show. Do you travel with him anymore?"

Bennett's smile faded. "He had to retire last year. He's not well. His arthritis is crippling. I don't think he'll ever sculpt again."

"That's terrible."

"I know. I miss him."

We walked in silence for a few moments.

"Well, you've convinced me about the sand," I said as we strolled north, this time along the edge of the water. A handful of hotels and a mix of condos and private homes stretched into the distance, up toward Cocoa Beach and Cape Canaveral, fringed by palm trees and sea grapes. I let the soft edges of a wave swirl around my ankles. "Ooo!"

"Feels good to me." Bennett's feet were awash in the wave, too. "Are you cold?"

"A little cold. But not frigid."

He laughed, and then I realized what I'd said.

"I think we've established that you're not frigid." Bennett caressed the small of my back for just a moment, his hand warm through the thin material, and then his touch was gone. But not before I'd felt a wholly different kind of shiver. A hot one that shot right to my lady parts.

I glanced up at him to find him staring at me. I sucked in a breath as he hastily looked away.

It wasn't going to be easy to keep this professional, was it?

"So you're a waitress and a wedding planner," Bennett said after a moment. "What other careers are you hiding?"

I smiled. "Not too many. I was recently a costumer's assistant at the Chamberlain Theater for the premiere of *Midsummer at Midnight*."

"Oh, yeah, I read about that — Jace Edison wrote that, didn't he?"

"Starred in it, too. And yes, I got to see him in his underwear."

Bennett laughed. "I'll never be able to compete with that." And then he fell silent, as if he'd caught himself saying more than he should have.

And I wanted to tell him to try. Try to compete. Jace hadn't interested me nearly as much as Bennett did.

"I also take a lot of art classes," I said, pushing my silly fantasies about Bennett aside. "I've tried photography, painting, sculpting. I'm taking a sculpting class right now, actually."

"You are?" His eyes flashed with delight. "So you're a sculptor like me!"

"Ha, no, I'm a student," I said. "A perpetual 24-year-old student."

"That's the best way to be. A student forever. Always learning."

"Except I feel like I should have a career by now. So do my parents," I added wryly.

"Careers are overrated."

"Isn't what you have a career?"

Bennett shrugged. "I suppose, but I never assume anything's going to last."

"That makes sense. Your sculptures don't last, do they? I think I'm drawn to art because I want to make my mark on the world. I just haven't found the right medium yet. I grew up in a funeral home ... "

"A funeral home?" His face scrunched.

"I mean my parents own a funeral home. It changes how you look at life. You see people facing the most stark reality of our existence every day: Life is short. That's one thing I know for sure. My ride on this planet is limited, and I want to do something that will leave a mark. Something people will look at for decades or centuries and love. Otherwise, what's the point?"

Bennett looked amused. "So you think my art is pointless?"

"That's not what I mean!"

"I think it is what you mean, but look. Making a sand sculpture and tearing it down after two or three weeks, or even a couple of months if I'm lucky and get a hotel gig, it's still making art. It's like a great performance. A ballet or a concert. It's still beautiful. It's still art. And it's still important. And even if it weren't important, if it gives people pleasure — if it gives *me* pleasure — it's totally worth doing."

"I can see that." I sighed. "At least you're making art professionally. And it *is* beautiful. I'm sorry if I sounded dismissive. Maybe it doesn't matter what I do. I usually end up helping other people with their projects. I'm like the perfect organizer. I keep the trains running on time, but I never get to blow the whistle."

He casually put an arm around my shoulders. And

even though I knew I should have shrugged him off, it felt so nice, I let him pull me a little closer as we walked.

"So far, I feel like you're organizing me very well," he said. "But if you want to blow my whistle, that's fine, too."

My face heated, but I couldn't help a chuckle. "You're laughing at me again."

"Laughing with you, Milia. Always laughing with you."

PART 2

*T*hanksgiving had come and gone, with another raucous family holiday at my parents' house with my three brothers and sister and bubbly nieces and nephews (two of my older siblings were married and popping out babies at an alarming rate). I'd met with Neil and worked out an initial cocktail menu, talked to the florist and made sure the invitations Thea designed were in the mail. Bennett was much on my mind, though I didn't see him again for a while; he had a sculpting gig in California. Just as well. I still had a lot of details to set up, and since everyone was coming down with holiday fever, there were countless distractions getting in the way of wedding preps.

It so happened that Bennett came back into town and insisted on a meeting with me on the same day I'd set up a tasting at Rafe's catering company with Alex and Sloane. I told him I couldn't meet him until afterward, but I still couldn't quell the tingle (jingle!) I felt whenever I thought

about seeing him again. I wasn't convinced I really needed
to meet with Bennett, but I didn't want to turn down an
excuse to have dinner with him. The mandate to have a
professional relationship had been eroding since that kiss
and had further weakened with each silly text he'd
sent me:

"I think you should put this on the wedding playlist.
Very romantic." With a link to one of my favorite holiday
tunes, "I Want a Hippopotamus for Christmas."

Or:

"I've been thinking about it, and I'd rather make a
sculpture out of whipped cream. Do you think Ralph can
deliver five tons of whipped cream? We can go swimming
in it after."

Or:

"Do you think the prince and princess should be
kissing in the sculpture? It's been so long, I can't remember
what a good kiss looks like. Maybe you can help me. We
can do it in the mirror so I can see you better. Did you ever
do it in the mirror? Kiss, I mean." With a smiley face.

To that one, I replied: "I've never done it in the mirror.
Kiss, I mean."

To which he replied: "Your qualification of your state-
ment has my imagination running wild. God help the next
person who hires me to do a sand sculpture. They might
have to surround it with a curtain and check IDs of anyone
who wants to see it."

I'd never engaged in a flirtation like this with anyone,
and it only whetted my appetite to see him again. And
scared me a little, because actually being in the same room

with him was a lot different from sending little notes. After all the double entendres we'd exchanged, I got hot just thinking about seeing him.

The late-afternoon sun poured golden light through the picture windows of Broussard's Catering and Patisserie in downtown Bohemia. It was a Thursday afternoon, a few days into December, meaning it was only three weeks until the wedding. Three weeks! In my increasingly frantic mind, everything felt like it was behind schedule, but Rafe seemed unperturbed as he smoothly laid out small plates of savories on the counter. His staff buzzed like bees in and out of the swinging kitchen door behind him, exchanging empty plates for full ones, as Brenda Lee belted out "I'm Gonna Lasso Santa Claus" on the loudspeakers.

The front of the shop was decorated to the hilt in Christmas, that kind of rococo Christmas of gilt and curlicues and more-more-more, with shiny gold and bright colors everywhere I looked. Tiered faux cakes with elaborate decorations were interspersed with gold-trimmed china place settings on display shelves. Gaudy angels spread their wings in the middle of the plates — the same angels, I realized, that adorned the windowsills of the decidedly less pretentious Double Diamond Diner. I had to suppress a chuckle when I saw them.

"Those steak bites with gorgonzola and arugula are fantastic," Sloane was saying as the plate in question was whipped away and replaced with bacon-wrapped shrimp and pretty cucumber-avocado bites.

"Just remember you need a couple of vegan options," Alex said. "Though I could eat that steak all night."

"So that's a definite yes on the steak?" I asked, scribbling in my notebook. *And points for arugula.* They'd liked almost everything so far, which would make it hard to narrow down the menu.

"Definitely yes," Sloane said.

"I love it when you say yes." Alex's gray eyes shone, and he leaned in and kissed her neck, just below her ear. Sloane's eyes closed, and her lips parted. I looked away for a moment, away from their intensity and toward the windows, and saw a flash of white sweep by and disappear. What was that? A sheet? A flag? A Christmas angel?"

Two women came in the door a moment later. It jingled merrily, enhanced with extra bells for the season, and they called out, "Happy birthday!"

Rafe looked up, puzzlement crossing his face before he brandished that tiny-tooth smile at them. "Ladies! Please make yourself at home at the table. I'll be with you in a few minutes." Then he hissed at the staffer exchanging plates on the counter, "Champagne for the Junior League, and bring out some of those cheese straws to keep them happy."

He turned back to Alex and Sloane with the brittle smile back in place. "I'm catering the Junior League Valentine's Day fundraiser in February, and they're here to sample some of our pastries."

"That's a great event," Alex said. "These cucumber things are delicious, and they should make the vegans happy. Can you add those to the list, Millie?"

"Sure," I said.

Two more ladies came in with a jingle.

"Happy birthday, Ralph!" one of them called as they headed for the dining table at the far end of the shop. There was no doubt this time. She was talking to Rafe.

He glowered before recovering his faux-pleasant smile. "Thank you, Janice, but it's not my birthday."

"That's not what I hear!" The well-dressed woman giggled, then called out to her friends at the table as they claimed glasses of champagne from the tray brought to them by one of the harried staff.

I began to have a funny feeling and looked back toward the windows. Nothing seemed out of place, but . . .

Jingle, jingle.

"Happy birthday, Ralph!"

"I hope you have some cake for us!"

"And I've been getting your name wrong all of this time."

Three more arrivals. And Rafe's face was three times as red.

"Thank you, ladies, but it's not my birthday! And my name is Rafe, of *course*." He said the last through a gritted smile, then turned to snap at another of his staff. "Bring out the cake samples."

I glanced at the door again. *There's no way Bennett had anything to do with this. And if he did, I'll kill him.*

But it was still funny. I coughed into my hand to cover a laugh at Rafe's constipated expression, then tried to distract the chef. "Thanks so much for bringing out such a variety of samples. I think we have plenty of great choices. I'll get back to you this week with our final selections."

"Wonderful," Rafe said, just as two more ladies came in.

"Happy birthday to you!" one of them began singing, and the rest of the group joined in. "Happy birthday to you! Happy birthday, dear Raaaalph! Happy birthday to you!"

Rafe's mouth opened and closed, evoking a gobsmacked goldfish.

"I'll be with you in just a moment, ladies," he said robotically. "Cindy?" he called to a nearby staffer, a petite blonde in a black chef's pillbox hat and jacket. I realized she was the sous chef I'd spoken with on the phone. "Could you help out these fine folks with the cake samples?" He turned one last time to Alex and Sloane. "I'm so happy we can cater your wedding. I'll be seeing you soon." He shook hands with Alex and disappeared through the swinging doors. A moment later, the unmistakable sound of yelling leaked into the lobby. I couldn't understand what Rafe was screaming, but maybe it didn't matter. He was pissed.

Cindy the sous chef smiled as if nothing was happening at all. She was probably inured to it by now, I thought. I had a feeling it wasn't the first time Rafe had yelled at his staff for little to no reason. She walked Alex and Sloane through the cake samples, and I took notes.

Rafe finally emerged and greeted the Junior League ladies, who'd been chatting and laughing and probably hadn't even heard his hollering. "It's Rafe, I assure you," I heard him tell them more than once, and I bit my lip to keep from laughing again.

When we donned our sweaters and jackets and left the shop — *jingle, jingle* — I watched the happy couple walk away. Alex had an arm around Sloane, and they were very much wrapped up in each other as they strolled down the street in the crisp, cool air. Above, the red, green and silver Christmas decorations on the street lights ruffled in the breeze, the tinsel fringe sparkling as the last beams of the sinking sun slanted down Bohemia's main street. But something made me stop on the sidewalk. Something different, off. I turned around to take a last look at the shop.

"Oh, my God." I put a hand over my mouth. A giant banner hung over the door, above the reach of the windows. On it were the words "HAPPY BIRTHDAY, RALPH!" surrounded by pictures of birthday balloons. Left of the greeting was a hilarious caricature of Rafe himself in a chef's hat, one finger in the air and a supercilious smile on his face.

"Do you like it?"

I spun to see Bennett lurking at the corner of the building.

"What the hell?" I walked briskly to him, grabbed him by the elbow and steered him down the sidewalk and away from the storefront so Rafe wouldn't see him. "I ought to smack you right now."

"Oh, please, baby. Smack me."

"Shut up! You're going to screw this up for me. He was furious, and I don't think he even saw the sign. You should have seen him."

"Was it good? How pissed was he? I made sure the

ladies saw it and told them how much Ralph loves birthdays."

I couldn't help it. I sputtered, and then I started laughing. Bennett laughed, too.

"He flipped," I said. "First he kept trying to tell them it wasn't his birthday. Then he tried to tell them his name was Rafe. And then he went into the back and screamed at his staff because he couldn't scream at his customers."

"Oh, I'm sorry to hear that," Bennett said through his own laughter. "Can you forgive me?"

"Maybe I can, but I doubt his staff will. How did you get the banner up there anyway?"

"The roof."

"Maybe I don't want to know."

Bennett pulled me into the alcove of the cigar store, where the sweet and musty smell of tobacco and the sound of Lou Rawls' "Merry Christmas, Baby" seeped through the door.

"Are you mad at me?" he asked softly, grasping my shoulders, his laughter easing into a slightly anxious smile.

"Yes," I said, but I was smiling, too. His eyes were indigo in the fading light, his lips plum. He saw my gaze drop to his mouth and return to his eyes, and his flashed. Flashed blue fire just before he yanked me against him and kissed me.

Gosh, Bennett was cuddly in a sweater. *Cuddly. Ha.* I remedied that impression in an instant. He was a fiery sun, a nucleus of heat. Of muscle, as he clutched me hard against him, his hands kneading my back through my thick sweater as his lips sipped mine. He tasted of peppermint. I brushed my palms along his scruffy beard, entwined my fingers into his hair.

"Mmm," he hummed as he tilted his head to take more of me, his chest crushing my breasts. My nipples pearled under my layers, not that he could feel them. But I could. They tingled, the way the rest of me tingled, my body singing to the tune of Bennett's delicious kiss. His tongue was sweet, slippery, hungry against mine. I opened wider, suddenly wanting much more of him, and damn the consequences.

"Pardon me, kids," came a gruff voice as the shop door opened and jingled next to us. A man who looked remarkably like Santa Claus (but in a green jacket) emerged with a cigar box in hand, followed by a cloud of smoke and the jazzy notes of the music. We broke apart with a gasp, letting him pass between us.

And then Bennett and I just stared at each other for a minute, breathing hard.

He took my hand, that mischievous look back in his eyes. "Dinner? Can we walk by Ralph Brucie's place again?"

"It's really Ralph Brucie? Not Rafe Broussard?"

"I don't know what he's done legally to his name, but yeah, that's how he was known back in the day. Come on. Let me see it one more time."

I nodded. I didn't let go of his hand. It was warm and strong and mine for the next few minutes. "Only if we cross to the other side of the street. I don't think I should be associated with you, at least not in his tiny little mind."

Bennett laughed. "Now you're seeing him the way I do. Let's go."

We crossed the street at the corner and walked back past Broussard's, admiring the banner. The light was fading now, and I wondered whether Rafe would even see it tonight. Did he go out his front door or the back?

It didn't matter. The joke had been pulled, and Bennett's grin was priceless as we walked by, heading toward my favorite Lebanese restaurant. His expression was all heat and light and humor. All things I'd been sorely lacking in my life. Not that this wandering sand sculptor could ever be a part of my life, not really. Could he?

Over beef shawarma, delicious rice studded with pine nuts and the world's most intense garlic sauce, Bennett told me about his latest sculpting job. But beneath the conversation was a subtext. His legs brushed mine under the table — his clad in jeans, mine in tights under my knee-length skirt, all the more sensitive to the feel of him. He touched my hand and joked with me, echoing his emailed quips and entendres, warming me to my toes.

"You sure you won't have a beer?" he asked as we were almost done. "Or wine?"

"I'm not really a fan of the wines here. It's the one thing they don't do well."

"Then somewhere else? Looks like there are a lot of cool bars downtown."

I frowned. "Do you want to get me drunk again?"

He grinned. "Would that be so terrible?"

"Yes," I said. "Probably."

"*Probably.* I sense wiggle room. Anyway, you won't get

drunk, because this time you've had a full meal and can opt out of those heavy-duty cocktails your friend makes."

"Though they *are* delicious."

"See? You want one."

"Wine," I said. "I'll drink wine. I know a nice place."

I took him to Plumeria Bar, with its luxurious red walls, suggestive floral photos, dark wood wainscoting and plush seating. We opted to sit at the bar, with its spectacular view. The wide windows behind the bartenders and the shelves of liquor overlooked Bohemia's small harbor, lined with boats glittering in the purple night. Many were strung with Christmas lights, reflecting off the water in an enchanting display of glowing colors.

"This is the good life," Bennett said over another beer, staring out at the boats.

I sipped a nice Oregon pinot noir. "You mean this?" I gestured to the bar, which was half-full and subtly decorated with fairy lights and faux holly. "Or maybe living on one of those boats? I've often wondered what that would be like, traveling the world, never staying in one place long. But I feel anchored to Bohemia."

"Traveling the world isn't all it's cracked up to be. I fly all the time, but once in a while I wish I had an anchor." He shrugged. "Then I get back to my dismal apartment, and I'm ready to fly again."

"I like Bohemia. I love Bohemia Beach, though I can't afford to live beachside yet. But it would be nice to have the option. Travel until I get my fill, then come back home to beautiful Bohemia Beach. Guess I need to figure out what I want to do when I grow up, first."

"You don't have to grow up." Bennett took another sip. "I'm living proof of that."

"But you have a career, even if you are a big goof."

"Hey!" He poked my knee. Then, holding my gaze, he touched it again with one finger, tracing a lazy little circle there.

I caught my breath. "Bennett."

"Yeah, Milia?"

"Are we heading down a road we shouldn't? I mean, with the wedding and all. You're my contractor. And you're already at risk of putting me in the soup with the caterer."

He chuckled. "See what you did there?" Now he rested his hand on my knee, squeezing lightly. Heat shot right up my thigh, warming places that hadn't been touched in forever.

"I'm serious," I said.

"So am I." His smile vanished. He released my knee and touched my cheek instead. "I know you're serious, because I can't see your dimples."

And then I smiled, because that's what he made me do. Smile. Against my will, or rather, turning my will, making me all too willing. Willing to smile, and more.

Bennett poked the resulting dimple and showed one of his own. "There they are," he whispered.

He leaned in and kissed me, right there at the bar, with a hint of ale and garlic and the peppermint from earlier. His fingers slipped into my hair, ruffling my bob, and then he let go and leaned back and watched me.

Could he tell I was a mess? All of my control, my fastidious devotion to self-improvement and schedules, had melted like a snowball in Miami.

What if I let this flirtation go forward to an obvious conclusion? And would it be a conclusion, the end of something? Or the beginning?

Would it destroy any chance of having a professional relationship if what we did now — tonight — was something else entirely, something terribly, wonderfully unprofessional?

Something hot and sparkling and tasting of peppermint and . . . sex?

I bit back a groan. I had had sex with exactly one guy in my life, that short-term boyfriend. Add in a few episodes of heavy petting and near-misses, and I was still severely under-experienced. And here I was entertaining the idea of bedding the expensive centerpiece of my friends' extravagant wedding, a wedding I had to execute in three weeks despite an ornery caterer and an even more ornery sand sculptor. Who was looking at me with magnetic blue eyes that should have evoked ice but instead glowed hot, like a searing gas flame.

He wanted me.

And I so very badly wanted him.

"I want another glass of wine," I said softly.

A slow smile spread across Bennett's face. "OK." He got the attention of the bartender and pointed to my glass, which the man refilled promptly before wandering down the bar to talk to a couple of women in elf outfits with tinsel garlands in their hair.

I took a long sip.

"You're drinking," Bennett said.

"Liquid courage."

"What do you need to be brave for?" His eyes never left mine.

I just smiled over the rim of my glass.

"This means I'll have to take you home," he said.

"I know."

Something came over his expression. Something dark and hypnotic and electric. Desire. It almost knocked me over. It went to my head faster than the pinot noir. It was so heady to be wanted like this.

"Bartender!" he called out.

"I'm not done yet."

"I know," Bennett said. "I just need a word with our guy." When the barkeep came over, Bennett leaned over and said something in his ear so only he could hear.

The bartender nodded. "No problem."

"What was that?" I asked when he went away again.

"You'll see."

Another beer materialized next to Bennett.

"Do you realize we haven't once talked about sand during this business meeting?" I asked.

"I talked a lot about sand."

"Your last job, yeah, but not this one."

"What do you want to know? I have my helpers lined up for the pound-up, a couple of strong surfer dudes who need a few extra bucks and will help me get it done fast. The equipment is reserved. The materials and sand are on order. I've done a more formal design drawing — I'll email it to you when I get home. We're ready to go."

"Oh. OK."

"You sound surprised."

"You said we'd need several meetings." I drank more of my wine. It was getting more delicious, and I was getting more relaxed. "So I thought there was more to discuss."

"Oh, I think we have lots to discuss." Bennett smiled again. "So much at the tip of my tongue."

Was it getting warm in here? Must be the wine. "Your tongue?" I licked my lips, an involuntary response.

His eyes caught the movement and darkened with wicked promise. "Yes. My tongue. Did you know that wine makes your lips even redder? And they're already like berries. Sweet. Plump."

I tried to make a joke of his flirting. "I don't think any girl wants parts of her to be described as plump, even her lips."

"But they look so delicious." He put down his empty glass, undeterred. "I want to lick away that ruby color and then nibble on them until it comes back."

"Hush," I whispered as the bartender walked by. I shot back the rest of my wine. Nerves. They got me every time. The wine somehow took the edge off.

"We could resume this conversation elsewhere," Bennett said in that buttery voice.

I nodded. "I think we'd better."

Bennett paid the check, and on the way out, he grabbed a bottle from the bartender.

"What's that?" I asked, floating now. Merry. Loose, but not so far gone as I'd been that night at The Junction Box. This feeling was rather pleasant. *Very* pleasant.

Bennett held the door open for me. "I had him hook me up with more of that pinot noir. It looked so good."

"On my lips, you mean?" I teased as we headed out the jingling door into the night. All the doors were jingling this December in Bohemia.

He laughed. "Especially on your lips. I bet it tastes good on your lips, too." He stopped us on the street and kissed me lightly, rolling his tongue along my bottom lip. I mewled at the carnality of it. So light. So lascivious.

Bennett's eyes darkened again, and he looped his free arm into mine. We walked toward my apartment building amid the holiday lights and sounds of music, Christmas and otherwise, pouring out of the bars and restaurants. There was no question for me now. Just anticipation. Nervous anticipation.

And good old-fashioned lust, as the warmth of his body ignited mine.

THE CHILLY AIR had sobered me up a bit by the time we reached my place, and I hesitated as I reached the top of the stairs and my door, Bennett right behind me.

I turned to face him. "I'm not sure."

He smiled. "Nothing has to happen here, Millie. Not unless you want it to. I wanted you to drink wine to make you happy, not to make you a pushover, to use your word. I want you to want me — want me sober or drunk or anything in between. Because in case it isn't obvious, I want you."

I wanted him, too, but somehow I couldn't say it. I touched his scruffy beard, then pressed my hand against his chest.

"What happens tomorrow?" I asked in a small voice.

"I don't know," he said. "Nobody knows. That's kind of the adventure of it."

"What if you just walk away? From me? From the project?"

"Ah," he said, grasping my wrist, moving closer to me. "You want to know my intentions? First, I never walk away from a job."

"Uh-huh."

"And I have no plans to walk away from you. I don't know what the future holds, but when it comes to you, I want to find out. Is that enough for now?"

For a moment I flashed on what we could be — future kisses. Future Christmases. He'd left the door open to any possibility. And that's all I really needed right now. Hope.

Hope and him.

I tilted my face upward in invitation, and Bennett covered my mouth with his, moving his lips over mine in a slow, intimate possession. He had me. I grabbed the thick knit of his sweater, a dark, mottled blue, and moved to push it over his head.

He broke the kiss with a chuckle. "Want to go inside first?"

"I — oh, yeah. Right." Embarrassed, I dug in my bag for my key and opened the door. I flipped a switch, turning on a neat little art deco torchiere I'd picked up at a yard sale. It softly lit my vintage sofa, chair, coffee table and checkerboard tile floor. My four-foot Christmas tree came on with the switch, too, its tiny colored lights shining in one corner. And on a small table by the window, an aquarium glowed, its two goldfish swishing contentedly as they circled the castle ruins in the middle.

"A castle!" Bennett said as he strode over to the tank. "But not made of sand."

I shed my bag and shrugged off my long cardigan, laying both on a chair by the door that acted as a catch-all. "If it were sand, it would have been long gone by now, and Bert and Ernie would have nothing to look at."

"That's the problem with art. You think it's forever, but sometimes it only lasts for a day." He smiled. "Got a corkscrew?"

"Believe it or not, I do." I retrieved it from the kitchen and brought it out to the cozy living room with a couple of wineglasses.

We sat on the couch. He got the pinot open and filled each glass to the brim, then raised his to mine. "To the magic of Christmas."

I couldn't help but laugh. "To caterers not quitting because of insane sand sculptors."

"That's awfully specific," he said, joining me in taking a sip. "That's more of a wish than a toast. Maybe you need a fortune cookie instead."

I shook my head. "I'm not a fan of fortune cookies. I don't believe in chance. We make our own luck."

"Oh, I think sometimes luck finds us." He clasped my free hand with his and brushed the back of it with his thumb. That low thrum of desire that had rekindled with his kiss on the landing pulsed upward again.

"Just a second." I got up and reached over to the lamp and turned it off, so only the Christmas tree and the aquarium lit the space.

Bennett's eyes shone. "Damn, Millie, you're beautiful."

"Oh, stop," I said, sitting and picking up my glass of wine. I took a big sip to hide my discomfiture.

"I mean it. Why are you shy?"

"I don't know. You make me shy."

"Why?"

"You're so good-looking, for one thing." *Oh, damn it.* The wine was working, obviously. The truth serum had kicked in again.

Bennett grinned and used one hand to brush my hair away from my face. "I'll never be as pretty as you. Trust me on this."

"Can I trust you?" I asked softly as he took my glass and put it with his on the coffee table.

"Of course you can," he whispered, taking me in his arms.

This time the kiss didn't stop. It began with the barest touch of his lips to mine, with the taste of wine, and unfolded, like the velvet petals of a deep red rose, unlocking, unfurling, silky and heady and sweet. He moved his mouth deftly over mine, coaxing me to open. I tilted my head and let him plunder me. Heat flushed through my body, and I moaned against him.

"Yes," he whispered as he paused to pull his sweater over his head. He had on a plain white T-shirt beneath, and I placed my hands against his chest, caressing the taut muscles through the cotton, the ridges and valleys. The feel of him was electrifying. He was mine, at least for tonight. I was doing this. I was glad. Blood ran hot through my limbs; fire flickered in my core.

Bennett eased off my flats and slid his hands up my tights-clad legs, slipping under my skirt to cup my behind.

"Oh, God," I said, letting my head fall back, losing control as he squeezed.

He kissed my neck, and fire ignited along my skin. And then his hands were on my blouse, unbuttoning, and I was yanking off his T-shirt. His chest was golden in the low light, muscular but not crazy ripped. He was lean and strong, temptation in the flesh.

While I was mesmerized by his body, he was taking inventory of mine, his hands sliding up my belly to caress my breasts through my pink satin bra. Before I knew it, he'd unhooked it, pulled it off with the blouse, and then my breasts were free, my nipples tight and sensitive under his caresses. He leaned forward and took one in his mouth, licking, gently pulling it with his teeth.

I groaned. I hadn't felt anything like this in ages. Perhaps never. I'd never wanted a man this much, of that I was sure. And his mouth on me felt like heaven, his suck-ing, his tugging, twinges of pain that only enhanced the avalanche of pleasure. He turned his attention to the other breast, and I reached for his jeans, unbuttoning, unzipping.

Bennett helped me get them off. *Holy shit.* If I'd had

any doubt about his desire for me, the tent in his briefs belayed it.

But he didn't take those off yet. He went back to kneading my breasts, watching my face, watching me lose control as the pleasure overwhelmed me, a half-smile of satisfaction on his lips.

"I was captivated by you the moment I saw you," he murmured, cupping the mounds of flesh, rubbing his thumbs over each pebbled peak. "I imagined what you must look like under that uniform. Your curves. Your pale skin." He licked one nipple, and I shivered. "Crimson on ivory. So hard for me. The reality is so much better than the fantasy."

Is this really happening? I let out a telling sigh as he leaned in to suckle my aching breast. He reached under my skirt to the waistband of my tights. With a hum, he released my nipple and focused on rolling down the hose. Every move, every touch he made heightened my arousal, until the tights were off and his hands again wandered under my skirt, touching me through my underwear.

I twitched as one finger found my nub through the satin, stroking me there. Then he pressed into my cleft through the damp fabric.

"Damn," he said, yanking down the panties. "Are you as wet as I think you are?"

Shamelessly, I clutched his shoulders and opened my legs, giving him more access, wanting him to touch me again. His little smile was back as he reached under my skirt and found my clit again, rubbing, flicking. Then he slipped his finger inside my slick slit.

"Oh, yes," he whispered. "Milia, darling, you are so wet for me."

"I want you, Bennett," I whispered back.

"The feeling is mutual. Do you like this?"

"Yes. Oh, yes." *Do I like it?* He was driving me wild, now sliding two fingers inside me, hooking them to stroke that spot that triggered a tremulous pleasure that built and built. I ground against his fingers, and he held me close before moving his other hand to my breast and squeezing my nipple. He caught my mouth with his, and I exploded, a shooting star, aflame with the ecstasy of his touch. I collapsed against him, holding him tight.

He kissed me just below my ear, igniting more sparks, and then he pushed me against the couch, swiftly removing my skirt so that I was naked before him. Vulnerable. But still so high on him that I didn't care.

He slid off the boxer briefs, and I sucked in a breath. His generous erection sprang forth, the head purple and shiny.

"Are you ready for me?" Bennett asked.

"I think so," I said honestly. I wasn't entirely sure. "Do you have a — a condom?"

He nodded, fishing around in the jeans on the floor until he came up with the packet. He ripped it open and rolled it on.

And then he leaned over me and tenderly kissed my lips. My eyes moistened. The emotion in that kiss — it wasn't just lust, was it?

He ended the kiss and held his shaft in one hand, guiding it to me. I opened my legs to him, and he slid his cock against me, stimulating my already sensitive nub. And then he pressed the tip inside.

I gasped at the sensation. It had been a long time, and I was tight. I knew it. Though I touched myself sometimes, I didn't have a vibrator. It was weird how new all this felt, even though I'd had sex before. And he was bigger than that first guy, too.

He felt so good.

"Goddamn, you are tight," Bennett said, echoing my thoughts. "Am I hurting you?"

"No. More."

"No more?"

"No," I gasped. "I want more."

His face was shadowed in the light, but the pure yearning in his expression was intoxicating as he pushed deeper into my wet heat, stoking the embers of pleasure. I groaned, and he suddenly thrust all the way in, all the way to the end of me.

"Yes!" I cried out. "Yes, Bennett. Again. More. Please."

"Oh, yes, my darling Milia," he said, and I smiled even as I moaned at his next thrust.

I made a lot of noise in the next few minutes. He drove into me with an escalating rhythm that had me lifting my hips to meet his, arching my back to take him in as far as I could. And then I was gone again, crying out, even as he cursed and rammed into me, holding himself against me as he shuddered in his release.

We melted into each other, replete. He rolled and pulled me on top of him, my small body against his larger one, and grabbed a fleece blanket off the back of the couch to pull over us.

"Sweet, sweet girl," he whispered in my ear, kissing my neck. "That was sooo fucking hot."

I giggled into his chest. "Yes, it was. Hard to believe it's December."

"Don't need a fireplace, that's for sure."

"But now I've been naughty, and Santa won't bring me any presents," I said.

"Angels have to fall to earth once in a while. Anyway, naughty girls get the best presents, don't you know that?"

"I always suspected."

Bennett laughed. "Good things come to those who are naughty," he said. "Coal is just a euphemism for fuel. Fuel for the fire. And you set me on fire."

Gratitude flooded me, a surprising emotion in the wake of our passion. But to hear him say I set him on fire was a deeply satisfying present in itself.

"Thank you," I whispered. I kissed him, happy to be the naughty girl for once. The nice girl kept the trains running on time, but the naughty girl got to have wine and orgasms and men like Bennett.

No, not men *like* Bennett.

Bennett. He was the one I wanted. And that realization sent a shiver through me at its power and improbability.

"Bennett," I whispered between kisses. "Bennett." As if saying his name would cast a binding spell. "Bennett."

Third time's the charm. Right.

And Santa's real, too.

BENNETT HAD to leave at dawn the next morning for a holiday festival in Orlando. He'd been hired to help sculpt a big sculpture by another team, and he needed to meet them early. Already dressed, he leaned over the bed, where we'd migrated last night, and gave me an all-too-brief kiss.

"I'll see you soon. Very soon," he said.

"Before the 22nd?" I couldn't help asking as I curled up in the blankets, wondering, as orange light eased through my windows, what the hell I'd done.

"Next week," he said. "As soon as I can."

Bennett kissed me again, and despite my tugging at his sweater, he laughed and left me. So much for me wondering if he had a work ethic. He either had one or was desperate to get out of my apartment.

"Oh, Pen, I'm such a pushover," I told Penelope later that morning in her apartment in an old house by the river, which is what most of us locals called the lagoon. She was hand-stitching crystals and tiny pearlescent beads onto the wedding dress while an eclectic mix of Christmas music played. Sloane was expected any minute.

"Pushovers have more fun," she joked. She glanced up at me, flipping her blond and pink 'do, then bent again over her sewing after shaking her head at my helpless expression. "You're going to ask me for guy advice, aren't you? I don't know why people always ask me about guys."

"Experience?"

"I may have experience, but I never learned a damn thing. I'm just lucky Jace came along when he did. There."

She stood, shaking out the dress and holding it up so it flowed in front of her.

"Hey," I said. "That's green, isn't it?"

"A very subtle green. Sloane wanted something a little different. It's very pale until the light hits it a certain way, and then it's this sort of lovely sea-green color."

"I love the crystals, too. And the barely-there lace straps and the tulle flounces below the knee. She'll look like a mermaid."

"She'll look gorgeous no matter what, and this color will really make her eyes pop. Plus the red and white bouquet will be amazing with this." Penelope put the gown on a hanger and stuck it on a crowded rack of costumes and dresses. "So what do you need advice about? Or should I say who?"

"I thought you said you couldn't give advice."

"Maybe not, but I want the gossip. And I'm glad you finally have a guy to gossip about!"

I rolled my eyes. "It's this guy I've hired for the wedding."

"Oh, God, not that caterer?"

"You know him? No, it's not him. It's — well, I'm kind of keeping what he's doing under wraps, but let's just say he's part of the entertainment."

"Ooo, is he doing something sleazy?"

I laughed. "No. But we're supposed to have this professional working relationship, and, um — "

"You slept with him, I take it. So what are you worried about? Ethics? Birth control? Was he awful in bed?"

"Ah, no, none of those things. He was incredible in

bed." I felt my face heat as she grinned. "But what if he blows me off? Will it be impossible to work with him?" *Or will he break my heart?*

"That's not what you're really worried about, is it?" Penelope asked, heading to the small kitchen, opening a couple of bottles of root beer and handing me one. The sweet fizz was a delicious comfort. "You're worried about how you feel right now."

"How do you know?" I asked, leaning against the counter.

"Because I've never, ever seen you lose your cool, even when the wheels were falling off at *Midsummer at Midnight* rehearsals."

"This guy totally makes me lose my cool," I admitted.

She smiled. "I think that's a very, very good thing. Knowing you, you wouldn't be losing your shit over him if you didn't have a really good instinctual feeling about him. Trust yourself. Trust your own judgment."

"But I think I lost all sense of judgment," I said as a knock came at the door.

"No, you haven't," Penelope said, walking over to answer it. "Sometimes you judge things with your gut. Go with it. I trust you, even if you don't."

"Hey!" Sloane said as the door opened. She and Cali walked in, bringing a breath of cool air with them and quick, happy hugs. "How are you? I can't wait to see the dress! Is it ready?"

"Ready for the wedding, no. Ready for your fitting, definitely," Penelope said.

Cali dropped her bag on the kitchen counter and

pulled out a camera. She popped on the flash as Penelope went with Sloane to retrieve the dress, and I took a sip of my root beer.

"You keeping up with your photography?" she asked me.

"Sometimes, but I keep being distracted by new projects. And lately, this wedding . . . "

"You were one of my best students," Cali said. "You have a great eye. You can apply that to anything, you know. But I hope you won't give up photography."

"I'll always shoot photos," I promised. "I'm just not sure it's the thing I'm supposed to do."

"You'll know. Like you know you have the right guy."

I looked hard at her. Could she read minds?

She chuckled. "I saw you with a cutie in downtown Bohemia last night. But you were across the street, so I didn't want to scream at you. Was it that guy who met you at the bar? Who is he?"

"I can't tell you." I bit my lip.

"Love is in the air. Or maybe it's mistletoe."

"Mistletoe! That's a great idea! I need to get some of that for this Christmas wedding."

"Definitely," Cali said. "You know it grows in the oak trees around here, right? Ask Sloane about the trees at her studio. She'll have to ask the doctors who own the big house if it's OK, but it's generally considered a parasite. I'm sure they wouldn't mind you getting some of it."

"It's up in the trees?"

"Yeah. You'll need a ladder or a pole or something. I

think some people use shotguns, but I wouldn't recommend that along the Bohemia riverfront."

I laughed. "Good advice."

Cali's blue eyes suddenly grew wide and bright as she looked over my shoulder. I turned to see Sloane step forward in her wedding gown. Her chestnut hair spilled over her shoulders, and her gray-green eyes leaned toward green with the help of the subtle color of the fabric. The bodice lifted her pale breasts so the sweetheart neckline enticingly enhanced her décolletage, and the satin flowed south, narrowing under a delicate rhinestone belt, hugging her curves until folds of pale green tulle swirled out below her knee. The gown sparkled, and so did she. I'd never been one of those girls who bought bride magazines and fantasized about my own wedding, but seeing this dress worn to such fabulous effect made me wonder what I'd look like in my own.

The flash went off, startling me out of my trance.

"Gorgeous!" Cali said, shooting a few more photos.

"What do you think?" Sloane asked me.

I smiled and shook my head. "You couldn't be any more beautiful. Though I've still scheduled the hairdresser and makeup artist for the big day."

"Of course you have," Sloane said with a chuckle.

"I need to add more sparkle," Penelope said, "but we're pretty close on the fit. And I'm glad you're not wearing those super-high heels for this. You wouldn't be happy with them in the sand."

"These are just great," Sloane said, poking out a graceful foot so we could check out her pretty white wedges. "I'm going to add a few red and green rhinestones. Comfortable and Christmasy. Oh, you guys." Tears were in her eyes. "I think I love the whole world right now."

"Aren't those the lyrics of 'The Christmas Waltz'?" Cali asked.

"Everyone's going to be in love with you," Penelope told her.

Sloane smiled. "Alex is enough for me."

Love. This was love. Not a couple of kisses and one night in bed.

But didn't love have to start somewhere?

BENNETT MADE plans to come over to Bohemia on Wednesday evening. It had been almost a week since I'd seen him, and I wasn't sure how I'd feel. Regretful? Distant? Annoyed?

He didn't give me a chance to think about it. As soon as I opened the apartment door, he crushed me in a kiss, kicked the door shut behind him and pushed me so far into the room we flopped on to the couch.

I pushed at his chest, nicely clad in a snug gray sweater, so I could grab some air. "Bennett! We can't do this now."

"Don't you like me anymore?" he asked with a faux innocent look, just before he started licking and nibbling at my ear.

"Oh, God. Yes. I do. But I have to run an errand, and then we have to go to dinner."

"Or I could just eat *you,*" he murmured in my ear

between licks and kisses, sending a lightning bolt right between my legs.

"I — I have to meet the caterer. It won't take long."

Bennett groaned, released me and adjusted his jeans. "Now there's the perfect mood-killer. Ralph."

I sat up, smoothing my short-sleeved, above-the-knee black velvet dress, which I'd bought just for our date. "You have to stop calling him that. Because then I'll slip up and call him that, and he will not be happy."

"But why do you have to meet him tonight?"

"It's just fifteen days till the wedding, and Rafe insists he needs more input on the design of the cake. Alex and Sloane told me to deal with him. I guess they've had enough."

Bennett nodded. "Not surprised."

"So I have to go."

"Why aren't you going to his shop?"

"Because it's closed now, and he said he has to know tonight. Something about ordering the right sugar molds in time for the right beach-themed embellishments."

"This sounds fishy." Bennett brushed my hair back behind the ear he'd just been kissing, and my skin tingled. "Does he have a thing for you or something?"

Was Bennett jealous? I could only hope. "He doesn't like me," I affirmed. "I think he despises me, actually."

"That won't stop him from making a pass at you. Especially in this cute little number." He ran a hand up my tights-clad leg and under the skirt of my dress, making me squeal and bat him away. But he made serious inroads into my willpower as he trailed kisses up my jaw.

"Bennett, please. A five-minute stop. Then we can go over to the beach for dinner. His house is on the edge of downtown. I'll pop in, pop out. And he won't even have to know you're there. In fact, I prefer it that way."

"Oh, you do, do you? Then maybe I'd better come in."

"Bennett, please."

"Just for a minute. You need a chaperone, and I'll be good, I promise."

I rolled my eyes. "If you do one naughty thing, you could ruin this whole event for me. Promise you'll be good."

"I thought you liked me naughty," he said in a husky voice, sending my temperature into the stratosphere.

"Later," I said, this time leaning in to kiss him. His tongue teased mine, and I broke away with reluctance. "OK?"

"Yes, ma'am," he said with a grin. And why not? He knew I was a sure thing.

I grinned back.

Bennett drove us to Rafe's address in his rough-around-the-edges minivan, which he said was pushing 200,000 miles. "Sorry the wheels aren't very sexy," he said. "I need this for work sometimes."

"It's sexier than my little car. And I like your lucky cat." The solar-powered cat on the dashboard, small and fat and white with a stoic expression on its face, waved one paw constantly.

"I picked him up in Japan. He waves even faster during the daytime. He makes me feel like I always have a friend on board."

There was something so vulnerable in Bennett's idle comment. *And could he be any more adorable?*

Rafe had a one-story house in a quiet neighborhood, probably built in the '60s, neatly landscaped and well-maintained with a screened-in pool in back.

I rang the doorbell, thinking I'd talked Bennett into staying in the van. Instead, as soon as Rafe opened the door with a "Good evening, Ms. Romano," Bennett popped out of the darkness behind me.

"Ralph!" he said. "I hope you don't mind me coming along. Millie and I had a business meeting."

To Rafe's credit, only an eyelid twitch gave away his displeasure. That and his icy tone. "I need to speak with Ms. Romano, and you will only get in the way."

"I've got to use the bathroom, so this will be perfect," Bennett said, pushing past us.

Rafe brushed at his unflattering black turtleneck as if Bennett had left a trail of goo on him, then ushered me inside. "It's at the end of the hall!" he shouted as Bennett disappeared into the house. "What a troglodyte," he said to me. "You're not keeping very good company, Millie."

So we'd gone from Ms. Romano to Millie, and he was lecturing me about my boyfriend — er, my — whatever Bennett was.

I put on the best smile I could manage. "Never mind him," I said. "Tell me what you need to know for the cake."

"Ah." Rafe's smile seemed as fake as mine, only more oily. "Please come into the kitchen. I have a few photos I'd like you to review."

I reluctantly followed him into the kitchen. It sparkled

with a recent remodel. Everything looked new — cherry cabinets, granite countertops, a huge top-of-the-line stove and ovens. Decorating the dining nook at one end of the long room, which flowed into a living area to the right, was a lighted cabinet with glass doors. All five shelves were filled with trophies. Some looked like trowels mounted to plaques. There were bundles of medals. Other trophies were more traditional metal cups, while a dazzling, faceted crystal bowl in the center dominated the display.

"These are from my life before Broussard's," he said proudly, directing my attention to the case. As if I would have missed it. I followed him out of politeness as he spoke. "Sand sculpting trophies are on the bottom. Your friend Bennett was never a match for me. The rest are ice-sculpting trophies. My proudest is the crystal cup, from a prestigious festival in Norway, where I 'iced' a dozen of the world's top competitors." He laughed at his own pun.

"Very nice," I said politely. "You had some cake decorations to show me?"

He cleared his throat, underwhelmed by my response. "Of course. Over here." His hand on my shoulder was unwelcome, but I turned toward the kitchen's central island, where a three-ring binder was open to photos of cake adornments.

"I wanted a little more guidance on which of these sugar pieces you'd like to see on the cake before I order the molds," Rafe said. "We have several but may not have the ones you need. There will be a small charge associated with these, but I'm sure you'll agree it's worth it to make the bride and groom happy."

I grimaced. *And to help you drain Alex's pockets.* I scanned the images, wondering where Bennett was. "The seashells are perfect, of course. Do you mind if I flip through?"

"Not at all." It seemed like he was getting closer to me. I could feel him behind me, and I didn't like it.

I flipped faster through the pages, then flipped back when something caught my eye. Jewels. I remembered what Alex had said about wishing he could decorate the ballroom in diamonds, and Sloane had those crystals on her dress . . . "How would you feel about mixing some jewels in with the seashells? It would match our theme." Our evolving theme. "Clear diamonds, red rubies and pale green emeralds to go with the color scheme. Oh, are these crystal snowflakes? A few of those would be pretty, too!"

"You have quite an eye, Millie. I can tell you're really in touch with your artistic side." He rubbed against me — on purpose? — as he leaned over and flipped to the next page. "How about pearls?"

"Can you make them look like pearls? I mean, not clear?"

"Of course. Iridescent, even. Lovely strings of pearls." His hand was on my shoulder again, squeezing, and he turned me toward him, leaning in close. I felt his hot breath on me before I realized he was about to kiss me.

I stumbled as I backed away. "I think that's enough!" I exclaimed. *On multiple levels.* "Those will be perfect. Do you have everything you need?"

Rafe straightened, his back rigid, his face pinched. "I think so," he said curtly.

"If you'll just show me out." I walked briskly ahead of him, out of the kitchen and toward the front door. "Did Bennett already leave?"

"If only I was that lucky," Rafe grumbled, escorting me to the threshold. We both peered into the darkness. The van was empty.

"Where could he be?" I murmured.

"Here I am. It was one of those things, you know?" Bennett said, emerging from the house, his arms folded awkwardly over his front. "You're going to need a new roll of toilet paper."

Rafe scrunched up his face in disgust as Bennett headed to the van.

"Thanks so much!" I told the caterer in as chipper a voice as I could manage, all while longing to kick Bennett. "Let me know if you need anything else. Will it be OK if I check on the ice sculpture early the morning of the wedding to make sure we have the proper display space set up for it?"

"Of course." Rafe's gaze was cold, in control again. "I'll look forward to showing you my *pièce de résistance*. Set up a time with Cindy."

"Thanks again." I followed Bennett down the steps. He was leaning into the van, fussing with something as I waited impatiently. Finally, he popped my door lock. Once I joined him in the van and Rafe had gone back inside, I turned to him. "What the hell were you doing in there?"

"What were *you* doing? He sounded like he was getting pretty friendly."

"Yuck. Way too friendly. I was just trying to get out with my dignity intact."

Bennett laughed, backing into the street and heading toward the causeway. "I left with more than my dignity."

I narrowed my eyes at him. "What did you do?"

"Don't worry about it."

"It's my job to worry about everything. If you did something to piss him off, it won't reflect well on me. I brought you here."

"Oh, he's used to taking a little shit from me. It won't hurt anything."

"What won't hurt anything?"

"Will you trust me?" He turned east, and we were on the road that led to the causeway bridge. Stars spangled a moonless black sky like snowflakes on velvet as he soared up and over the water toward the barrier island.

"I could've used you in the kitchen. He was like an octopus."

Bennett shot me a dark look. "Did he touch you?"

"Not in any way that mattered." I shuddered. "Not for lack of trying."

"I'll kill him."

"Please don't! I dodged him. He got the message. I need this to be successful. I need you to know how important this is to me."

"I know," Bennett said. "Don't worry. I've got your back."

I wondered if he knew that he had all of me, despite my inner martinet, who was demanding discipline and freaking out about details and deadlines. I looked over at his profile, at his scruffy beard and his strong hands on the wheel and his merry eyes as he sang along to Brenda Lee's "Rockin' Around the Christmas Tree" on the radio. He was like a ball of fireworks going off all at once, noise and light and chaos and danger, and somehow, despite knowing what was good for me, I just couldn't turn away.

I forgot about Rafe and focused on enjoying our dinner at a beachfront restaurant with a view of the ocean. We couldn't see all that much through the windows, just the lights of ships on the horizon and the ever-shifting glimmer of the dark sea. But we could hear it. Accompanying the restaurant's piano-jazz Christmas tunes was the calming, primal sound of the crashing waves, a rhythm as old as time. Older than sex. I couldn't stop thinking about sex, apparently. It occupied one of my habitual streams of thought but kept crowding its way to the forefront when Bennett grinned or laughed or teased me or touched my hand. By the time we'd finished dinner and wandered out to the beach, I was crazy for him.

This is what comes of too much deprivation. When you finally get some, you can't get enough.

His arm was around me as he led me down the beach and away from the dim lights and noise of the restaurant. Soon we reached one of Bohemia Beach's oceanfront parks, the beach empty and chilly and beautiful as my eyes adjusted to the darkness. I marveled at the display of stars overhead. I'd had two glasses of wine, not enough to make me drunk. If I was drunk on anything, it was the stars and Bennett.

"They don't hold a candle to you," he said. We stood by

one of the wooden staircases that nestled up to the dunes, leading to an invisible parking lot. I was tilted back against him, looking up, trying to pick out constellations. I turned to face him, and he caught me up in his arms.

"The stars are eternal," I said.

"Not really. They started with a bang and will end with a whimper, or so I'm told. Who's to say you aren't as eternal as they are?"

"Or aren't."

"We don't know. It's a beautiful mystery, what's beyond those stars." Bennett pulled me close. He grazed my lips, teasing, stirring the embers inside me into fire. His tongue slipped inside my mouth, so delicate, so insistent, tangling with mine. Suddenly the chill was gone. I tugged him closer, and his tentative touch became demanding, his body pure heat, his taste pure sin. He pulled me under the stairs, slipping one hand under my dress, cupping my ass as he ravaged my mouth.

"Not here," I said, breaking the kiss, breathless.

"No one's here, and even if they were, they can't see us. Trust me. I'll keep you safe, my angel, my darling Milia." His hands were busy under my dress, easing the tights off, rolling them down. As he slid down my body, he kissed my neck, my cleavage, my belly through the soft velvet. He made no move to remove my sweater or lift off my dress; in fact, he only rolled the tights to my knees. But then he was kissing me down there, through my panties, before he pulled those down, too. It was all happening so fast, and I was too delirious to think about stopping him. He licked my clit, and a shiver wracked me. I clutched his hair as he began teasing me in earnest, stirring riotous quakes of sensation with that devious tongue of his.

"Oh, God," I hissed, backing against one of the wooden posts that held up the stairs, hoping it would hold me up, too.

"Mmmmm," he hummed, holding me by the hips, crumpling my velvet dress as he sucked at my bud and licked it again, his nimble tongue dancing on that needy bundle of nerves, circling, prodding as frissons of heat and pleasure radiated from that tiny sun at my center.

With the sound of the waves and the breeze came the sound of voices, and I froze as someone — two someones — walked on the boards above us, on the landing, chatting about the cool weather. But Bennett just chuckled softly against me and resumed his licking, dipping his tongue into my cleft and rolling it against my nub again. I couldn't help myself. I had no control here. How freeing to have no control.

He sucked hard on that nexus of pleasure, and I convulsed against him, bucking against his mouth. The tension fled from me, and I shook against the rough post and yanked his hair and bit back a cry as I came so hard, tears fled my eyes.

Bennett kneaded my behind as he continued to lick, teasing out every last drop of bliss until I nearly collapsed against him. He caught me, stood, held me up against the post and kissed me deeply, tasting of salty sex, sea air and him, with a hint of whiskey from the cocktails he'd had over dinner. And I wanted to taste more of him, all of him — but unlike him, I wasn't brave enough to do it here, under the steps with tourists above and the ocean crashing just a few feet away.

The voices were gone now, the footsteps in retreat.

"Bennett," I whispered as he paused in his kiss and ran a thumb across my swollen lips.

"Are you OK?"

"I can't even tell you how far beyond OK I am," I said softly. "But if they'd come down those steps . . . "

"Shhh. They didn't. Would you want me to take it back if I could?"

"No." I threaded my hands in his hair and kissed him hungrily. "No. Don't ever take it back."

He chuckled and kissed me again before he helped me get my clothes in order so we could go back to my place.

PART 3

*T*he next several days were hot and cold. Hot
with Bennett, cold in Bohemia — a Florida cold
snap, with highs in the 60s.

Bennett no longer needed excuses to come over from
Orlando to see me, and when I indulged in a day off, I
went to his place, a surprisingly spare one-bedroom apartment. I got to know his bedroom really well that day.

In the back of my mind, I wondered at my own hedo-
nism. I'd never wanted a man so much, never lived so
much for pleasure. The organizer in me was still at work,
but she found it so much easier to take an hour off here or
there when Bennett was involved. Twinges of guilt for
those stolen moments faded with each day, each kiss.

We'd decided he didn't need a hotel during the
wedding. He'd stay at my place. The idea made me
nervous. It wasn't like he was moving in, but even two or
three nights seemed almost like a commitment. Through
the nerves, though, I was giddy. Embarrassingly giddy.

Down, Millie, down, I kept telling myself every time he sent a thrill through me. Which was pretty much every other minute I was with him, and every second I was with him in bed.

I got a phone call early on the Monday before the wedding, just before my shift at the Diamond, that made me second-guess all that giddiness. The ID indicated the call was from Broussard's Catering. Unfortunately, it wasn't Cindy, through whom I'd been arranging most of the details.

"Ms. Romano, I am not happy," Rafe said as soon as I answered the phone.

Uh-oh. "Why? I mean, what can I do for you?"

"Keep your sand 'artist' away from me, and if you're wise, away from you as well."

"Has he done something to offend you? I'm sure he means well." I wasn't sure of that at all, but there was no way I was going to confess complicity in whatever he'd done.

"Ask him, and mark my words. Having him involved in this wedding is courting disaster — for both of you."

"Everything is going beautifully," I said as soothingly as I could. "We're all very excited about the menu and the cake and, of course, that gorgeous ice carving. Is it still OK if I stop by the morning of the wedding to get a sense of its size?"

"I can send you the measurements."

I swallowed my annoyance. Sloane might want to be surprised by the décor, but there was no way I wanted to be.

"It will be better if I get a look in person to get a feel for it in three dimensions. We wouldn't want to set up any floral arrangements or anything else in such a way that they hide your masterpiece, and we also want to frame it properly."

Rafe mulled my words for a moment. "That's sensible," he said, sounding somewhat mollified. "Cindy said you planned to come in at seven. Don't be late. I have a lot to do and some items to pick up before the staff comes in to finish the cooking."

"Of course, and thank you so much," I said. "I'm sure it will be brilliant."

Maybe I was laying it on thick, but he seemed to take my forced compliment as his due. "I'm certainly more of an artist than others I shall not speak of again."

He was starting to tick me off, but I bit my tongue. "May I speak with Cindy about a couple of the details?"

"Just a moment." It sounded as if he'd laid the phone down on a hard surface. I heard the buzz of people working, and in a minute, Cindy picked up.

"Millie?" she asked. "I hope His Highness didn't chew too big of a hole out of your ass."

I barked out a laugh. She didn't usually talk like that. Rafe must've been out of earshot.

"It's OK. What I want to know is, what exactly pissed him off?"

She chuckled and lowered her voice. "He didn't tell you? It was pretty priceless. A package arrived this morning at the bakery, a big cardboard box marked 'frag-ile' addressed to Chef."

" 'Fra-gi-le. Must be Italian.' "

Cindy laughed at my *A Christmas Story* reference. "I love that movie! Well, there wasn't a leg lamp inside. It was lined with packs of dry ice. Inside it was another box, wrapped in pretty foil paper and ribbons. It was heavy. I wondered how it could be fragile. It was also cold as fuck, because he cursed when he touched it. I touched it, too. A bunch of us gathered around to watch him open it. We all thought it was some kind of gourmet delicacy kept cold for shipping."

"And it wasn't?"

"It was a solid block of ice with something very special at the center. We almost couldn't tell there was something in the middle of it at first."

"I almost don't want to know." Inside, I was planning ways to beat Bennett with one of his own shovels.

She laughed again. "It was that stupid crystal bowl Chef is always bragging about. The one he won for some ice sculpting contest. It looked like part of the ice. He was livid once he realized what it was. 'I knew he took it. I *knew* it,' he said. Of course, he'd spent the previous few days bitching about his maid service — he thought they'd broken it and thrown it out or stolen it or something."

"So I guess he didn't notice it was missing right away," I said, remembering that night Bennett accompanied me to Rafe's house. "Are we sure a maid didn't take it?"

"It had a gift tag that said 'Merry Christmas, Ralphie.' After that, Chef couldn't stop ranting about how horrible and evil your sand sculptor is. The block of ice is taking up one of our sinks while the damned thing melts."

I couldn't help it. I laughed. And then I remembered how angry I was at Bennett. "I'm sorry if Rafe took it out on you."

"Oh, Chef takes everything out on us," Cindy said cheerfully. "Good training for when we all move on to real restaurants. I'm getting out of here next year, I swear."

"I wish you luck. And thank you for giving me the scoop."

"No problem," she said. "Don't worry about Thursday. It's going to be perfect."

"OK. See you then." I hung up. The truth was, I did worry. I worried that Rafe would tear out Bennett's throat. Or worse, screw up the wedding.

Maybe not worse. When I thought of Bennett's throat, I thought about kissing it. I'd given the man a hickey last week. A hickey! I'd never done that in my entire life, and I kind of wanted to keep on doing it.

At the same time, I really wanted to kick Bennett's ass. He was making my job much more difficult, no matter how funny his prank was.

I'd have my chance that afternoon, after my shift at the diner. He was staying with me tonight so he could get the forklift early tomorrow and meet the sand truck and his helpers at Trifles for the pound-up. They'd spend the day packing the sand in stacked boxes that he'd already taken over to the restaurant complex and would quit in time for Alex and Sloane's pre-wedding party that night. I'd already invited him. Now, given his latest stunt, I wasn't so sure that was a good idea.

When Bennett knocked on my door at three, I'd only

just pulled on jeans and a sweater after a post-Diamond shower. I was exhausted, but seeing those deep blue eyes twinkling energized me. Until I remembered what a pain in the ass he was and frowned.

"What's wrong?" he asked, stepping inside and closing the door. He kissed me on the cheek. "Tired?"

I shook my head. "Tired of your antics. Can you guess who called me today?"

He smiled sheepishly, but his eyes glinted with glee. "He couldn't have blamed you."

"I guess he didn't feel like looking up your phone number."

"No, he knew I would laugh at him, so he called you so he could elicit the proper contrition."

"And why in the hell is it my job to apologize for you? You know how important this job is for me. Yet you keep antagonizing the guy."

Bennett gently rested his hands on my shoulders. "You didn't say you were sorry, did you?"

"No, because I had no idea what you'd done, at least not until Cindy told me."

He grinned. "Was it awesome?"

I let out an exasperated sigh and shrugged him off, heading to the kitchen to pour myself a glass of wine.

"Uh-oh," Bennett said. "You're drinking. Must be serious."

I took a sip and put the glass down. "Bennett, you're hilarious, and Rafe is a jerk, and I appreciate the dynamic. It's just that your timing couldn't be more awful."

His gaze darkened. "He's long overdue for a bit of humbling, in my opinion."

I scrunched my brow, puzzled. "What is it between you two? Why do you hate him so much, and why do you have to fuck with him on my dime?"

"I'm sorry." Bennett moved into the tiny kitchen and poured himself a glass, too. "I never should have pulled that prank with the trophy, but it was so irresistible. The perfect storm of his arrogance and my opportunity."

"You said you had my back. But I'm just not sure if I can trust you."

"Absolutely, you can. Or should I say ass-bolutely?"

"I'm not that drunk yet," I said drily. "But I might be later."

"I sure hope so." He kissed me lightly on the mouth. "Can you forgive me?"

I shook my head, and then I nodded. I already had.

He smiled broadly, put down his glass and kissed me more thoroughly.

"But you owe me," I said. "I hope you're ready for some action, because I'm going to work you hard."

"Oh, baby, that sounds so good." He leaned in to kiss me.

I put a finger up to his mouth to stop him and seared him with a wicked smile. "We'll see if you say that in an hour."

❄

"THIS WAS NOT what I had in mind," Bennett said from the top of the ladder.

He wore a jacket over his sweater and had been bitching about the cold for the past thirty minutes. But maybe that's because he was twenty feet up an oak tree behind a large historic house on the river next to Sloane's pottery studio, clinging to that rickety, borrowed metal ladder, beating at branches with a rake.

"There's a bunch!" I said as a large clump of mistletoe fell to the ground.

"Is that enough?"

"No. I think we need at least three more so I have enough."

"There aren't that many goddamned doorways in the ballroom, are there?" He looked down at me, and I couldn't help but giggle. Late-afternoon sunbeams danced through the leaves and cast a halo around his head. Even annoyed, he was handsome.

I tugged my scarf closer around my neck and hollered back. "There's going to be a photo booth, and I need some for that. I promised the florist I'd give her some to add to the centerpieces. We're going to put some on the arch on the beach for the ceremony. And — "

"Oh, for God's sake." Bennett shifted position and whacked another branch to no avail. He moved up a few more rungs to the tippy-top and reached higher, to the other side. He swung the rake with force and smacked a particularly large bunch. It fell in two big clusters. He looked down at me and held up the rake, as if to say, "Is that enough?"

Just then, the ladder started to sway.

"Bennett!" I screamed.

"Shit!" He dropped the rake, and I jumped out of the way as it bounced to the ground. He reached out as the ladder tilted, grabbed a branch and desperately clung to the ladder with his feet. Somehow he hooked his foot into the top step and inched the ladder over until it settled against the trunk.

He gingerly moved one foot down a rung, testing. The ladder held. "I'm coming down now, if that's OK with you."

"Please do." I held my breath as he eased down the ladder halfway, then deliberately slid the rest of the way to the ground. He bent over, put his hands on his knees and took a few deep breaths.

I went to him and put a hand on his shoulder. "You OK?"

He straightened and looked at me. And then he smiled, a slow smile that warmed me up more than my jacket or my scarf or, heck, the summer sun. "Were you worried?"

I dropped my hand and gaped at him. "Were you *faking?*"

"No. I really could've fallen on my ass. But I was OK. Especially when I surmised how upset you might be if I fell."

"You're something else."

"I know." Bennett looked down at the ground and then back into my eyes. "I'm sorry about all the shenanigans with Ralph. I didn't mean to make things harder for you. He's just such a tempting target. I know that's no excuse, but believe me, I have my reasons for screwing with him."

"As long as you promise not to do it again before the wedding, I'm willing to move on."

"I won't. I absolutely promise. In return, can I please stay on the ground?"

I giggled. "Yes. You were a trouper. I have plenty of mistletoe now."

"Still lots left above us, though." Bennett reached a hand behind my head and pulled me in for a fast, hot kiss. "Guess that means we have a lot of kissing to do."

"Well, I'm not doing it here. Can you return the ladder while I scoop up the mistletoe?"

He brought the ladder and rake back to a shed behind the house while I stuffed a big tote bag with all the mistletoe we'd harvested. With its thick stems, deep green leaves and translucent white berries, it looked nothing at all like the plastic stuff they sold in the discount stores.

"I ordered pizza. We should beat it home," I said as we got into my car.

"You're big into the details, aren't you?" Bennett asked. "The pizza. The mistletoe. This whole crazy wedding."

"That's my curse." I drove onto the river road and started wending back toward downtown Bohemia.

"Why is it a curse?"

"Because sometimes it feels like I'm going to spend my whole life planning other people's events without ever making great art or having an adventure of my own."

"Have you considered that what you do is an art? An amazing and important art?"

I huffed. "Don't try to make it more than it is."

"I'm serious. Without people like you, so-called 'art'

wouldn't happen. You had that theater job — the costumes wouldn't have happened without you."

"I don't know — "

"This wedding wouldn't have happened without you. My beautiful sculpture wouldn't have happened without you."

I laughed. "It hasn't happened yet."

"It will!" Bennett said. "And all because of you."

"Not *all* because of me. I mean, let's get real. You're the sculptor."

"But you're the instigator," he said as I parked in the tiny lot behind my apartment building. "Art never happens without a plan. Otherwise, it's just a spark that goes out. Inspiration without perspiration. An individual can make art happen, sure, but it's people like you who make it bigger. Who help it reach the world."

We got out of the car, and I chewed on his words as we entered my building and went upstairs and into my apartment. "I think there are a lot of artists who would scoff at what you're saying."

"You know what? Anyone can have artistic talent. You do, judging from the bits and pieces of your work that you've shown me," Bennett said. "A lot of art never sees the light of day. You can be a fucking genius and labor in obscurity your entire life. You can have a day job and create great art at night and hope someday you'll make it. Or you can reach the next level — your art can be *seen,* with luck and timing and help. Your art, my dear Milia, may be a marriage of talents. You can make art, but you can also make things happen. That's an art, too."

The pizza arrived. Bennett paid, and I grabbed a beer for him and a root beer for me.

"All that stuff about making art happen sounds good when you say it." I got a couple of plates, and we sat on the couch and each grabbed a slice. "But I still don't think planning a wedding is making art."

"Then look at it this way." He put down his plate and reached for my hands, forcing me to put down my plate, too. "Do you believe in fate?"

"Fate's kind of like magic. I don't really believe in magic."

Bennett held my gaze. "When you help make art happen, you are enabling fate. Making magic."

I raised an eyebrow at him.

He smiled. "More to the point, do you enjoy planning stuff? Making things happen?"

I cocked my head and considered the question. "I do. Actually, I love it. I didn't get an associate's degree in business just because I thought it could get me a job. I really get satisfaction from this kind of work. It just doesn't feel as important as art."

"I think maybe you've been looking at your life all wrong." Bennett squeezed my hands and released them, took a sip of his beer.

"Oh, really?" I couldn't keep sarcasm out of my voice. I took a bite of my pizza and eyed him skeptically.

Bennett chuckled. "Yeah. You can still make art even while you're conjuring that make-it-happen magic. Both things make you happy. And maybe both things will make you immortal, you never know. But you said it yourself —

life is short. Do what makes you happy. How many people can say they do what makes them happy? It's a gift. In this season of gifts, accept it as yours."

"Sounds like you're trying to get out of giving me a Christmas present."

He laughed, kissed my cheek and resumed eating his pizza. I flipped on my small TV, and we finished our dinner while watching *White Christmas,* with all its bright colors and snappy patter. Maybe he was right. In fifty years, would I be around? In a hundred years, the way things were going, would humanity be around? Nobody knew the future. This movie that so many people loved, made as a forgettable entertainment and now a staple of holiday TV, might have been forgotten, too, except for what Bennett called fate. Might still be forgotten. How much art survived the centuries? Maybe the greatest art was making the most of the moment.

Clad in their red and white furs, the cast of the movie sang the finale as snow fell in the background. In the light of the little Christmas tree and the aquarium, I flipped off the TV and turned to Bennett. I leaned into him, cupped his face with one hand and touched my lips to his. He responded with heat, encircling me in his arms, moving his mouth fervently over mine, taking my breath away.

"You know what?" he murmured between kisses. "You make me believe in fate."

Emotion overwhelmed me. *What is he saying?*

He kissed me again, and I forgot the question.

❄

AFTER RUNNING WEDDING-RELATED ERRANDS, I entered the Trifles ballroom at midmorning the next day to the air-rattling sound of large power tools. In the corner where the sand sculpture was supposed to go, Bennett was driving a forklift with a bucket attachment, dumping a load of sand into a wood form built inside a larger, lined, half-assembled sandbox that would help keep sand off the floor. One of the surfer-dude helpers was using a hose to wet the sand, while the other moved slowly over the pile with a power compactor, packing it tightly. All of them could have modeled for ancient Greek sculptures, and none of them were wearing shirts.

I lost myself in admiring them for a moment until Bennett was done dumping a load of sand. He looked up, saw me and smiled, turned off the forklift, then waved at the dude with the compactor until he turned it off. "Take a break, guys."

"About time," that dude said as blessed quiet returned.

"Hey, you had a break two hours ago."

"I didn't know four hours could feel so long," Dude Number Two said.

Bennett dismissed them with a gesture. "We have two more layers to add to this, and we have to get it done by five, so you'd better get used to the idea. Go get a soda at the cafe and come back in ten. Tell them to put it on my tab."

The guys picked up their discarded T-shirts, shrugged them on and went out the big loading door where Bennett had brought in the forklift.

"You have a tab?" I asked.

"Seemed like the easiest way." He climbed out of the machine.

"That's some pile of sand in the parking lot."

"Yeah, I don't think management was very happy with our five-ton mountain this morning. I promised them it would be gone by the end of the day."

"Will it?" I looked dubiously at the ten-foot-wide, two-foot-tall octagonal box they'd created. It was almost full. More two-foot-high wood walls were stacked near the door, awaiting assembly for the upper tiers.

"No problem," Bennett said easily. He caught my gaze wandering to his pecs and arms and back up to his face, and he grinned and walked over to me. "I wish we had more than ten minutes."

I laughed and placed my hands lightly on his chest, running them up to his shoulders. His skin was sweaty and sandy and I didn't care. "I barely have ten minutes myself, but I wanted to make sure you had what you needed and it was going OK."

He slipped his arms around my waist and pulled me in for a deep, thorough kiss. He smelled of sweat and spices and tasted of peppermint. I felt a little dizzy when he let go. He always made me crazy, but now, as he radiated scent and heat from his physical work, my body had a primal response.

"Maybe I should go," I whispered.

"Maybe you should, before I ravish you in the sandbox."

"Sounds uncomfortable."

Bennett grinned. "Probably. Sex on the beach is always grittier than you think it's going to be."

I shifted, not wanting to picture him with anyone else. "I wouldn't know."

He kissed me lightly. "We can remedy that sometime. Maybe in a nice little hut on the water on an island somewhere, with champagne and nothing but the sound of the waves to keep us company."

That was better. I'd rather think of a future with Bennett than his past, however wildly improbable a future seemed.

I took a step back and shifted my bag on my shoulder. "I texted you the directions to Alex and Sloane's condo. You can make the party tonight, right?"

"Ass-bolutely," he said, and my face grew warm. "I hear he has a killer wine collection."

"That's true. We can get started on that champagne tonight."

"Sounds great." He kissed me again, just as the surfer dudes came back in the room and whistled.

When Bennett let me go, I was half-embarrassed, half-drunk on lust. "I'll see you at seven," I said hoarsely. "You have the key?"

"Got it." He held my gaze and smiled. "I'll clean up after this mess and see you there."

"OK," I said softly, answering his smile.

As I left, I heard the surfer dudes clapping and Bennett good-naturedly telling them to shut up. The roar of the tools began again as I got into my car.

Why did I feel shy? Maybe it was because it was the

first time Bennett would be hanging out with not just me, but my friends — even if they didn't know what he did yet, given I still wanted to surprise the happy couple with the sculpture. Or maybe it was the idea of Bennett having a key to my apartment. It was a little too much like having the key to my heart, and we hadn't had any kind of conversation like that. This was a temporary arrangement, but how I longed for it to be more.

I delivered mistletoe to the florist, grabbed fish tacos at my favorite burrito shop, then headed to Alex and Sloane's. Her gang of friends was meeting there to assemble the favors for two hundred guests, and I wanted to help. And supervise, just in case.

I brought the supplies with me in a bunch of barely manageable large bags, feeling like Santa. I buzzed the condo once I was in the elevator. In a moment, it lifted me toward the eighth and top floor, all of which was occupied by the couple's home.

It was my first visit. Seemed like I was always working when Alex and Sloane had one of their parties.

The elevator opened into a foyer decorated in a mix of antique and modern, which led me to a vast living area populated by comfortable furniture and large, modern paintings. Far across the big space, sliding glass doors led to a balcony overlooking the sea. In front of the doors, a white twig tree was adorned with white lights, red ribbons, seashells and stunning crystal snowflake ornaments.

"Over here, Millie!" I heard Penelope call. I found her, Cali, Thea and Ez at a dining table hidden behind a pillar and a screen of plants and statuary. They were sipping champagne and helped themselves to a platter of colorful Christmas cookies at the center of the table while The Waitresses' "Christmas Wrapping" played from hidden speakers.

"It's a good thing you came before we got completely drunk," Cali said.

"Speak for yourself," said Ez. "If being in a band has taught me anything, it's how to hold my champagne."

"Not me." Thea's red curls shook with her laugh. "I'm already tipsy."

"Eat more cookies," Penelope said, "before I do."

"I brought them here so I wouldn't eat them!" Thea said. Everyone knew Thea couldn't cook, but her occasional baking binges were worth waiting for.

I put down my bags on the floor, grabbed a sugar cookie and took a bite. "Oh, my God, Thea, these are good. Where's Sloane?"

"Getting stuff ready for the party tonight," Penelope said. "We felt like she shouldn't have to make her own favors. Since we can't be proper bridesmaids, it's the least we can do."

"You're all doing more than most bridesmaids do."

"Except a bachelorette party," Penelope pointed out.

"She didn't want one," Cali said. "So tonight we have a little something planned for her." The others chuckled.

I looked around at their grinning faces. "I feel like maybe I should know what that is?"

"I think even you should be surprised at something from this wedding," Ez said, refilling her glass. "Don't worry. Alex is in on it, too."

"OK." I let out a little sigh of relief. If he was OK with it, it couldn't be too wacky. "I've got all the stuff we need." I started emptying the bags onto the table. "Two hundred telescoping roasting forks, marshmallows, shortbread cookies — those will take the place of graham crackers — four hundred organic dark chocolate squares, snowflake-spangled clear bags, lots of ribbon, and wedding match-books, just for fun. Enough stuff for every person to make two s'mores. We'll put two marshmallows, four cookies and two chocolate squares into each bag with a match-book, tie the bags off with red ribbon and tie the bags to the forks. Ready?"

"Two hundred favors?" Ez groaned. "I'm going to need a lot more champagne."

"Did someone say champagne?" Sloane appeared in the doorway, dressed down in leggings and a long knit shirt, holding two bottles beading with condensation. She laughed when she saw the pile of stuff on the table. "I'd better bring you a cheese platter, too."

"Now you're talking," Cali said. I joined them at the table, gave in to a glass of champagne, and we dug in to our task.

There was a really good feeling among this group. Even though I wasn't as close to them as they were to one another, they were warm and funny and totally welcom-ing. I hadn't had enough girlfriends in my life. I'd been too focused on other things. I vowed to myself that was going to change, starting right now. So I had another glass of champagne and told them I was bringing a guy to the party tonight.

By the time they were done teasing me, giving me advice and raving about the benefits of their own boyfriends, I was comfortable and happy with them and terrified at what was at stake for me. They were all paired off. I had a feeling I was just impaired.

When the caterers arrived with the real food (not from Rafe's company, I noticed), it was just in time to save us all from being completely looped on champagne. The favors were done and stowed, and we all dove in to the buffet as the rest of the guests started to arrive.

I'd just softened my inebriation to a pleasant buzz with an assortment of delicious appetizers when Bennett appeared. I sucked in a breath.

He wore relaxed gray jeans, a black jacket and a button-up white shirt, open at the collar. Somehow the lack of color in his clothes made the blond streaks in his brown hair pop, and when he turned those blue eyes on me, I almost ran across the room to him.

I held my own by the food table and waited for him to come to me. He smiled, reading me, I thought. Sensing how I felt. How much I felt.

He leaned in and kissed me. "Nice place. I guess they can afford me."

I grinned. "Yeah, but don't get any ideas. Even Alex said he can't afford diamonds all over the ballroom."

"I deal in quartz, not diamonds. Tiny, tiny quartz." Bennett looked more closely at my eyes. "Are you drunk?"

I smiled, took his arm and led him to the balcony doors. "Just a little fizzy."

"Oh, good." He slid the door open for me, and we both went out.

It was pleasantly cold. I'd been running around all day in a casual tunic and leggings with a long sweater, but I'd taken the sweater off while we were working on the favors. Now I shivered, and Bennett put his arm around me as we looked over the railing at the beach below us. The ocean's muted roar was comforting, a counterpoint to the Christmas tunes. A waxing moon high above made the sea foam glow, and fairy lights lined the railing.

"How did it go today?" I asked.

"We finished the pound-up. I got rid of most of the sand mountain, but I'll have to do some sweeping in the morning before the venue's managers get a good look at the parking lot. And then I have to sculpt the hell out of it."

"Do you feel good about it?"

"Ass-bolutely." Bennett grinned.

"That reminds me," I said through my happy buzz, "you need a drink."

"Let me taste some of yours first." He sipped at my mouth, then kissed me more deeply, wrapping me up in his arms, cozy and warm. Dreamy and delirious, clutching his neck, I got lost in his kiss, wishing we were back at my place instead of at this very public party.

"You taste delicious," Bennett finally murmured as we came up for air.

"So do you."

"You haven't tasted all of me yet." He wiggled his eyebrows.

That's about when the champagne started talking.

"I want to taste you right now," I whispered. "All of you. I want you in my mouth."

"Fuck. You're killing me." He searched my eyes and kissed me again, claiming me. "I want to get out of here right now."

"You have to eat. And I have to see what the girls have cooked up for Sloane."

"You're driving me mad," Bennett said. "I never thought you'd be the one who drove me this crazy."

"I'm not really sure how to take that," I said, selectively mulling the phrase *the one* and not daring to hope what he might mean.

"It's a compliment, I promise you."

A shout went up inside the condo. We went back inside to see the guests gathering around Sloane as she sat on a low stool in the center of the living space. Ez's guy Gary and Cali's brother Damien — in an outrageous green velvet suit trimmed in zebra-print fur — rolled in a large, wrapped present on a dolly and settled it in front of the bride. It had a strange shape. Sloane looked over her shoulder at Alex as they took the dolly away.

"Is this what I think it is? You gave me a new one last Christmas."

Alex looked as if he were trying not to grin but couldn't help himself. "Open it."

Sloane smiled and shook her head and started tearing off the red ribbon and green foil. "It *is* a pottery wheel," she said as she tore off the last shreds. "Wait a minute. This is my pottery wheel from the studio!"

"Yes, it is," Alex said.

"What are you up to?"

Alex nodded at Ez, who stopped The Ventures' "Sleigh Ride" on the music player to switch to a different song. The familiar strains of The Righteous Brothers' "Unchained Melody" filled the room, and Sloane's mouth dropped open.

"I understand you refused a bachelorette party and told Cali 'absolutely no strippers,' " Alex said to laughter. Sloane turned pink. "And I also understand you really hate a particular scene in a particular movie."

"*Ghost,*" Sloane lamented, and there was more laughter.

"Oh, my love," Alex said. "My darling, you are not getting out of it that easily." And he pulled his sweater over his head to the roar of the crowd to reveal a muscled torso that any stripper would envy. The women whooped. Damien whistled.

I was laughing, and then I was agog at Alex's naked chest, and then I laughed again as Damien pulled up a chair behind Sloane's stool and Alex sat on it. Gary, a potter himself, plopped a blob of wet clay onto the wheel, plugged the machine into an extension cord and flipped it on.

"I'll get you for this," Sloane told Gary.

"Revenge is a dish best served cold," Gary said with a wink. He tossed back his curly hair and joined Ez by the stereo, laying a big smack on her lips.

"Sloane! Sloane! Sloane!" the crowd shouted.

"Go on, make something!" Cali said. She had her camera in hand and was snapping photos as the song evoked the famous scene in the movie.

"Oh, all right," Sloane said, pressing the pedal to make the wheel spin. She slapped her hands on the gray clay, centering it, shaping it.

The roar went up again as Alex slid his hands over hers, kissing her neck, sliding the wet clay up her arms. She began laughing, laughing and crying as she got more and more goopy. Her clay was a misshapen lump, at least in part due to Alex's awkward movements, and finally she gave up and turned around, grabbed his face with two clay-covered hands and kissed him, to the delight of the guests. Then she slid her muddy hands down his chest and tweaked his nipples.

"Ouch!" Alex shouted to laughter. "OK, my love, my darling. I just wanted you to know how special you are to me. And how grateful I am that you aren't sitting on some oily stripper's lap right now."

"Never," Sloane said with a smile, kissing him again. The crowd applauded, then dispersed to eat and drink and chat as the guys made the pottery wheel disappear and the couple vanished into their room.

"Guess they have to clean up," I said.

"Or get dirtier," Bennett replied.

"Can't really blame them." The sparks in the couple's eyes were unmistakable.

"I'm going to eat now," Bennett said, "and maybe drink, and then we're getting out of here."

Thirty minutes later, he'd bundled me into his van with a stolen bottle of champagne, saying he had a surprise for me. He drove beyond the turnoff to the causeway and pulled in to the parking lot of one of the big oceanfront hotels.

I shot him a sideways glance. "I thought we didn't get you a hotel room?"

"I got a hotel room."

"Oh." Did he want to escape me that badly? Did he need an out, just in case?

"I got it for us. For tonight. Something special and fun, since tomorrow I'll be really exhausted."

"Oh." My vocabulary was seriously stunted right now. "That's nice."

"It's very nice," he promised in a low voice.

We had no luggage. It was just us and the champagne as we entered the tenth-floor suite. Its view of the Atlantic was even more dizzying than the condo's. And it had an enormous bed.

A wave of worry washed over me.

"Bennett?" I asked as he opened the champagne and filled a couple of flutes. "Is this — this thing between us — is it just about sex?"

He put down the bottle on the bar and turned to face me, a calm and curious expression on his face. "Is that what you think it is?" He picked up the glasses and handed me one. "I haven't analyzed it, but it's not just sex. I want to be with you. Don't overthink it."

"Overthinking is what I do," I said wryly. "I want to be with you, too. The truth is, I'm a little out of control around you."

"And you don't like being out of control." He smiled, a wicked smile that cracked me open like a walnut. "Drink."

"I will, because I want to. Not because I need champagne to get in the mood. I don't." I took a deep sip. "I'm drunk around you with or without champagne."

"Hearing you say things like that makes me want to tear your clothes off."

Hearing his words, seeing him so handsome in the low lights of the beautiful hotel suite, I lost the thread of my worries.

"You don't have to tear them off. I'll help." I smiled back at him, turned and walked toward the bed. I took another sip of my champagne before I put the glass down on a nightstand and turned toward him.

He followed, prowling like a cat, watching me. I'd rarely taken the initiative in our affair, content to let him lead me into pleasure. Now he seemed fascinated. Intense.

I shrugged off my long sweater, letting it pool to the floor, then kicked off my shoes and slipped off the leggings. The tunic top remained, fluttering around my body as I moved toward Bennett.

I pulled it over my head and let it drop to the floor.

"Oh, sweetheart," he whispered. He set down his glass on a nearby table and reached out to touch the red satin bra, to run his fingers over the lace trim accenting the plump curve of my breasts. He ran his hands down my waist to the matching panties, stretching the fabric with his fingers.

"Not yet." I reached up and eased his jacket off his muscular shoulders, letting it drop to the floor. I popped open the top button of his shirt, and then the next and the next, slowly working my way down until I could pull it off his shoulders, too. I ran my hands over his beautiful muscles, his tanned skin. I leaned in and licked one of his dark, flat nipples.

Bennett sucked in a breath. My hands moved down his torso to his pants, unfastening them. I dropped to my knees and pulled them down and off with his socks and shoes. Finally, locking my gaze with his smoldering one, I drew off his briefs.

His cock sprang free, hard, curving slightly, pointing toward his waist. I'd seen it many times now, but not from this perspective. Even on my knees, I felt a heady rush of power. It came from the way he looked at me, desperate, hungry. I ran a hand along his length, from his tightened balls to the moist tip. Then I took him in my mouth.

Bennett's groan gave me almost as much pleasure as the taste of him. I stopped thinking and only felt, lost in the sensation of his hot shaft filling my mouth, sliding in and out against my tongue, hitting the back of my throat; of my body thrumming in response to his undulations against me; of the aching need growing between my legs.

"Enough," he croaked after a few minutes. He touched my hair, pushing me ever so slightly back. "Enough. You'll make me explode. I want you first. I want to be inside you."

I released him and let him pull me to my feet. He kissed me hard, feverishly, and I moaned against his lips. He stripped off my bra and panties, then he reached for his discarded pants and pulled a condom from the pocket, tearing it open, rolling it on.

He whirled me and threw me to the bed.

Bouncing on my back, I laughed, breaking the seriousness of the moment. He smiled — right before he pushed my legs wide, clambered over me and thrust into my wet passage.

"*Yes!*" I grasped his arms and arched.

"I won't last long."

"Fuck me, Bennett. Fuck me hard."

He growled in response and drove into me again, again, again. I didn't stop making noise until I came, shuddering in transcendent spasms around him. He followed me, crying out, clutching me against him until we both stopped shaking.

We collapsed against the bed, panting, hot. Dimly I heard the ocean as I curled against his chest, burying myself in his arms. Bennett pulled the covers over us and stroked my back until my breathing eased.

"Darling Milia," he whispered into my hair, just before I fell asleep.

Jostling. Bright light. A loud voice.

"We have to wake up. Millie. Millie!"

I rolled over. It took me a second or two to remember where I was. This bed was much more comfortable than mine. "What?"

"It's ten o'clock already! I have to start my carving, not to mention get the rest of that sand out of the parking lot. Shit, I can't believe we slept so late."

Oh, crap. His words penetrated the fog. It seemed like a blink since our lovemaking. But the big hotel room was filled with morning light, and the ocean outside glittered in the sun. I realized that the centerpiece of this beautiful wedding was horribly behind schedule, and it was totally my fault.

But damn, Bennett looked good as he whipped his clothes on.

"I've got some old clothes in the van," he said. "I'll drop you back at Alex and Sloane's so you can get your car, but then I've got to get over to Trifles."

"I'll follow," I said. "I'll sweep up the rest of the sand while you work."

"OK." I was surprised he didn't argue. Bennett looked genuinely alarmed.

I used the bathroom, then found my clothes and dressed quickly. "Is it really that bad?"

"I should have started three hours ago." He shook his head. "I'll get it done, but I wish I hadn't slept so late."

"I have confidence in you." But I was flashing back on all my concerns when I'd first hired him. And here I was, screwing around right there with him. Literally.

We finished getting dressed and got out of there. Bennett left me at my car with a quick kiss. I buzzed the condo, and Sloane let me in to pick up the favors we'd made the day before. She insisted on making me a cup of coffee, and we talked over wedding details for a few minutes before I could escape and head over to Trifles.

I found Bennett in shorts and a T-shirt in the ballroom. He'd already removed the wooden forms from the top layer of sand. He glanced at his sketches as he stood on the next tier and chopped away at the sand with a small shovel, making rough shapes that would become the heads of the prince and princess.

"The broom is in the corner," he called out, "if you want to sweep away that extra sand in the parking lot. It's not too bad."

"No problem."

"And Millie?" He paused in his work and looked up, showing me one of those smiles that had first attracted me. Only with something poignant behind it, a flash of the real Bennett who'd cannonballed into my life. "Thank you."

I nodded, smiled back and headed to the parking lot for cleanup duty. All in a day's work for a wedding planner, I supposed. At least one who was sleeping with the talent, with the wedding just one day away.

BENNETT HAD BEEN RIGHT. He was exhausted.

I'd checked on him once in the late afternoon after running all my errands, and he'd been hyper-focused on his work. The heads had emerged from the sand in beautiful detail, and he was shaping the middle level, but I could see there was a lot left to do.

He kept working as I ran more errands and checked off items on my to-do list: Get checks from Alex for all the vendors. Go over a shot list with Cali and Wyatt, who were shooting photos, and Gary's cousin Kayla, the videographer. Make sure I had the marriage license and that the officiant was ready to go. Double-check the seating arrangement against last-minute cancellations. Confirm table-decorating details with Trifles and the florist.

Finally, I dealt with a hysterical phone call from the

hair stylist and found a different makeup person, since her cosmetologist friend had suddenly flaked and ridden off to Vegas on a motorcycle to get married to her biker boyfriend. Which sounded a lot easier to me.

When Bennett got back to my place around nine that night, he was dead on his feet. He'd grabbed fast food for dinner and took a few minutes to have a beer with me — as I sipped iced tea, not ready to risk something more fun — before he collapsed into bed.

He assured me the sculpture was on target, but his anxiety was evident. When I'd finished my work and slipped into bed next to his gently snoring form, that worry kept me up later than it should have. And I had to get up early and go to Broussard's to check on the ice sculpture.

For the second morning in a row, I was awakened by Bennett's anxious voice.

"Millie. Millie!" A big, warm hand shook my shoulder, and I rolled over to give him the stink-eye. "I'm sorry, but the van won't start. Can you give me a lift?"

"What time is it?" I rolled again and reached for my phone. Just then, the phone alarm went off with Les Brown's brassy big-band rendition of "The Nutcracker Suite," and I almost had a heart attack. "Shit!" I turned it off.

"It's 6 a.m."

"I can *see* that! I have to be at the caterer at seven. No way I can get ready, get you to Trifles and get there in time, and I absolutely can't be late."

"Then I'll ride with you."

"If Rafe sees you within ten feet of me, his head is going to explode."

"I'm willing to take that risk," Bennett said. Then he grinned.

I rolled my eyes. "All right, all right. You can wait in the car while I check out the ice sculpture. It should only take a minute. I just have to make sure it's going to fit where we've planned it and that it doesn't show an orgy or anything like that."

"Where has this dirty imagination been, and can I see it more often?" He kissed me as I sat up, shaking the sleep out of my head.

"You bring it out of me."

"Excellent." He kissed me again.

I had to push him away, though I didn't really want to. "Make yourself useful. Run down to Sugar Shack and get us a couple of coffees. I'll be ready in twenty minutes."

"Yes, Milia, darling." He left the apartment as I stumbled into the shower.

Twenty-five minutes later, with wet hair and a bad attitude, I was snug in my leggings, kick-ass boots, tunic top and long sweater, ready for the day's tasks. The plan was for both of us to come back to my place later and change before the wedding. The ceremony might have been ten hours away, but it felt terrifyingly close given what we had to accomplish.

We wolfed down the delicious doughnuts; the coffee came with us as I drove Bennett, his bag of tools and my bags of wedding favors to the parking lot behind Broussard's Catering and Patisserie. Pre-dawn pink filled the sky over Bohemia; streaks of narrow clouds tinted with yellow and orange carried no threat, only a gentle reminder that summer's storms were a long way off. It was going to be a cool, beautiful day. Weather was one thing a wedding planner didn't have control over, and I was grateful.

We were a few minutes early, and the lot was empty except for a couple of catering vans. I got out of my car, and so did Bennett, coffee in hand.

"Where are you going?" I asked.

"Just enjoying the fresh air."

"You're not coming in with me."

"I know." He managed to sound a little hurt.

My mouth quirked into a half-smile. "You don't really want to talk to Rafe, do you?"

"Ralph? No, of course not. I'll behave and stay out here and, I don't know, do some hand warm-ups."

"That sounds dirty."

"It could be."

I chuckled just as a silver Lexus pulled into the lot, making me think of those irritating ads that showed people getting cars on Christmas morning with big ribbons on them. This one didn't have a ribbon, just Rafe, looking cranky. He emerged in crazy green pants with Santa heads all over them and a red golf shirt adorned with a Broussard's logo. And those bright green Crocs, of course.

"Thank you for being prompt," Rafe said to me, then clenched his jaw when he realized who was next to me.

"You go ahead." Bennett nodded at me, trying to head off Rafe's incipient outrage. "I'll stay here."

Rafe's face changed, became unreadable. "You think you're funny, Westyn, but your jokes are just a pathetic attempt to make yourself feel better in the face of superior talent."

"I'm sure that's it," Bennett said mildly, sipping his coffee.

"You just can't get past the fact that I'm always going to win, can you?" Rafe sniffed.

Admirably, Bennett said nothing, but I could see cold anger glint in his eyes.

"Hey, guys, you're both incredibly talented," I said, trying to ease the tension. "And I can't wait to see the ice sculpture."

"Ever hear from Nina?" Rafe asked Bennett.

A muscle ticked in Bennett's jaw. "She shows up at an exhibition now and then."

"Dumping that tart was so satisfying. Because *she* certainly wasn't. You should be glad I took her off your hands."

My stomach did a queasy flip as Bennett blanched. What had Rafe done?

"But that's all over now," Rafe continued. "Would you like to see what real talent can do? Come in and see my ice sculpture."

"I'll see it later today," Bennett bit out. "I have work to do."

"I think you should see what you can aspire to," Rafe insisted. "See it now while it's still frozen and perfect."

The chef wasn't going to let go, now that he had hold of the bone. Now that he had Bennett cornered in some way I didn't understand. I widened my eyes at Bennett and tipped my head toward the building. *Just make him happy. For five minutes.*

He slowly nodded, his eyes dark and angry. He put his coffee in the car, and we followed Rafe to the door.

It sounded a two-tone electronic alarm as Rafe unlocked it, like a particularly nasty doorbell, and he keyed in a security code just inside. Then he took us through a back hallway by a large pantry and a crowded storage room before we entered the kitchen proper. He flipped on more lights and a sound system that started playing holiday music while I took in the large, impressive work area. Long stretches of stainless-steel counters. Shelves of pots and pans and implements. Multiple stoves and ovens, big refrigerators and a walk-in freezer.

"Cindy will be putting the finishing touches on the cake this morning, so I can't show you that yet," Rafe said, "but the ice sculpture is ready to go. We'll bring it over this afternoon when we move in to the kitchen at Trifles to finish and stage the food."

"Excellent," I said.

"Come on in." Rafe held the metal door of the freezer open. "It's a little nippy, but it kind of gets you in the Christmas spirit, doesn't it?" He sounded strangely giddy.

"Sure does," I agreed, trying to be chipper as Bennett and I entered. My breath made little puffs of steam. Bennett crossed his arms against the cold. Despite his sinewy build, he seemed fragile. He wore just cargo pants and a T-shirt, ready to work on his sculpture, not expecting a detour to the North Pole.

"This is it," Rafe said, flipping on an overhead light. The single bulb glimmered on the sculpture.

I tried not to gape.

"I'm sorry you chose to be with this brigand, Ms. Romano," Rafe said, "but I'll take it from here. Goodbye."

"What?" I whirled away from the hideous sculpture to see the freezer door slam shut.

Bennett rushed to the door, tried to open it. It wouldn't budge.

"Don't those things have a safety release?" I asked.

He shook the door handle. "If there is one, it's not working. Ralph! Rafe!" Bennett shouted. "Let us out! Now!"

"This is bad," I said.

"Let us out!" Bennett shouted. "You've proved your point. Open the door!"

"What point?"

"Does it matter? I just want the dickhead to open the door."

But there was no response, and distantly, I heard the electronic bell rigged to the back door sound its horrible *WAH-wah.*

A shiver passed through me. I looked at Bennett, my sympathy evaporating as I realized just how horrible this could get. We were locked in the freezer with our lives on the line and a wedding to stage. At that moment, I wasn't sure which was more critical.

"You. You made this happen."

"Me?" Bennett threw up his hands. "Why are you blaming me?"

"If you hadn't kept goading him, messing with him — "

"Millie. Calm down. We'll make it in time."

And there we were, as previously mentioned, trapped in the freezer. I spat nails at Bennett, who claimed he'd have no problem finishing his sculpture when we got out.

"*If* we get out," I said after we'd argued for a few minutes and he'd tried, unsuccessfully, to calm me down. From their platform, the hideous icy mermaid and merman loomed over us, their kiss frozen, their nipples ridiculous. Around us, shelves were filled with frozen meat and other food. Nothing helpful like, say, a crowbar. Nearby, big blocks of clear ice awaited their fate. Kind of like us.

"We will get out." Somehow Bennett, as pissed as he was, had reacquired his calm. "Frankly, we have to get out."

Whatever cool I normally wielded had been shattered by the sound of that door locking us in. "I know. I have a zillion things to oversee for the wedding!"

"Not the first thing on my mind," he said. "We could die in here."

I blinked and pulled my sweater tighter. "Freeze to death?"

"Or suffocate. Frostbite first, probably."

"Oh, great. Thanks. Great."

"He's just pure evil," Bennett said.

"Who? Rafe? Don't change the topic."

"Ralph. Ralph the asshole."

"What did he do to you anyway? Who's Nina?"

Bennett shot me a narrow glance and didn't say anything.

"Well? Secrets, Bennett? I've told you everything about

me." I shook my head, realizing how far gone I was over this guy. "What the hell have I been thinking? I let myself be distracted by you. Let myself — " I blinked back tears. I didn't want them frozen on my face. "And now this wedding is screwed." I paced the short floor, lost in my rant. "Oh, my God. Alex and Sloane. I really didn't want to disappoint them."

"She was my fiancée."

My head snapped up. "What?"

Bennett looked tired. Sad. "Nina. My fiancée. He seduced her. Dumped her."

"OK, wait a minute. A couple of things here." Dazed, I tried to get my points in order. "First, you said you hadn't ever had a serious relationship."

"I said nothing came of my relationships."

"That's not exactly how I interpreted it. And you knew that."

"Why does it matter to you, anyway?" he asked, angrier now.

"It matters. It fucking matters. More than you know." Tears filled my eyes in spite of all my attempts to hold them back.

"Millie — " His eyes were stormy with pain, reflecting mine. "I was barely twenty-one, young and stupid. So was she, apparently, but I couldn't see that, couldn't see that all we had was a few laughs between us and a mutual need to belong to something. I was so lost back then. I was still traveling with Gerald but breaking out, sculpting my own stuff. He tried to talk me out of getting engaged, but I thought I knew everything." Bennett reached out, touched my shoulder.

I shrugged him off, not ready to process what he'd said, and went to stand on the other side of the ice sculpture. "Point Number Two: How could Rafe seduce anyone? He's a weasel. I knew it from the first time I met him."

"Have you ever known one of your girlfriends to date a weasel? Have you ever met a guy who seemed like Mr. Wonderful until you realized he was the devil himself?"

I took a deep breath. "Maybe."

"That was Rafe. Ralph. He has an ability to put on a facade that's pretty convincing if you don't know him well. He talked her out of being with me and got her into bed. She and I have barely spoken since."

"You seemed pretty upset at what he said."

"That's because I hate *him*. I hate what he did, but I don't hate that I'm not with Nina anymore. In a way, Ralph is right. He did me a favor. Though I didn't much want to be with any woman for more than a night or two after that. At least until now."

I looked at him through the upside-down heart formed by the ice sculpture's mermaid tails and let out a sob.

He rushed around the sculpture and wrapped his arms around me. "I'm sorry, Millie. I'm sorry I got us in here. You're right. It's my fault."

I didn't deny it, but I didn't push him away, either. My anger dissolved, and I held him tightly, sharing his warmth, needing him. *Oh, God. I needed him.*

"Do you have your phone?" he asked after a moment, still holding me. "Mine's in the car."

"So is mine, in my bag. I didn't even lock it. I didn't think we'd be in here long."

"If they don't come back for the sculpture until this afternoon, this could be very bad for us. Hypothermia at least."

"And the wedding — "

"One crisis at a time, darling Milia," he said, sounding more like his confident self. He released me and brushed a tear off my cheek. "We have to not die first."

I sniffled. "OK. Good plan."

"It's not a plan, but it's a goal."

He went back to the door, jiggling and banging and yanking. It didn't budge. Finally, he stopped, panting, and I went to him, wrapped my sweater around our shoulders like a scarf and held him. He enclosed me in his arms. It wasn't much warmth, but I wasn't sure what to do next.

"Hey, Bennett," I snuffled into his T-shirt.

"Yeah?"

"Can you do something about those nipples?"

"These?" He reached between us and squeezed my breasts.

"No, you idiot." I snickered. "On that stupid sculpture. Even if we don't live to see the wedding, I don't want the happy couple blinded by the headlights."

Bennett laughed and stepped back, then looked up at the mer-couple, thinking. He poked around and found a box of tools on the lower platform of the table that held the sculpture. In a moment, he came up with a hammer and small chisel.

He held them up. "Just the tips, or breast reduction surgery?"

"The tips would be fine. We're going for PG-rated."

"Done," he said.

It only took him a few minutes with the chisel and another tool or two. When he was finished, the boobs were almost tasteful. The rest was debatable, but it would have to do.

He came back to me, embraced me. The chattering of my teeth eased, but the cold crept into my bones as the time ticked by. There was no clock, and we didn't have watches or phones, but I guessed at least fifteen more minutes passed as we huddled together, each lost to our own thoughts.

"There's a safety release on the door, but it's broken," Bennett finally said, stepping back to rub his arms. "Rafe absolutely knew that."

"Ass-bolutely."

Bennett smiled grimly. "He *is* an ass. An evil ass."

"The worst. Doesn't he know he could kill us? I mean, this would be murder, wouldn't it?"

Bennett scowled. "I don't intend to die today. If we could find some tin foil, maybe we can wrap ourselves up. Preserve our warmth."

"Like frozen baked potatoes." I paused. Something had changed. "What's that?"

"What?"

"Listen!" I admonished.

Silence.

Bennett was shivering. "I don't hear anything."

"Somebody turned the music off. Somebody's out there!"

We both started screaming and shouting and banging on the door. A minute later, there was a clanking metal noise, and it opened.

Thank Santa and the reindeer, it opened!

Cindy was there in her chef's jacket, her blond hair tucked under her pillbox cap. She looked at us in disbelief as we dashed out. "What in the hell were you doing in there?"

"Freezing to death," Bennett said.

"Almost," I amended. "Your boss locked us in there."

"He knows that latch is broken. I've been bugging him about it for months." She didn't seem to ken that he'd done it deliberately. "People die in freezers every couple of years, you know. It's a real problem."

"We're acutely aware of that now," Bennett said. "And we have to go."

"Yes, we do." I hugged Cindy. She felt warm. The kitchen felt warm. And outside was Florida! "Thank you. Thank you so much. I can't wait to see the cake."

"It'll be great!" she said, still sounding puzzled as we dashed for the back door. "See you later!"

"IT'S A LITTLE AFTER EIGHT," I said as I pulled in to the Trifles parking lot. "That's not so bad, is it?"

"I wanted to be here by six, and even that might have been pushing it," Bennett said, all seriousness now. He grabbed his bag of tools, and we headed into the ballroom.

The Trifles staff had deployed a fleet of round tables, but they weren't even covered yet. The stage was set up but empty. And the half-finished sand sculpture was conspicuous in its giant sandbox in the corner, detailed on the top and lumpish on the bottom.

Bennett turned to me. "You're taking a sculpting class, right?"

"I've taken two. Just finished one."

"That pretty clay figure in your bathroom is yours, isn't it?"

"Yes." Anxiety rippled up my spine. "And you are not asking what I think you're asking."

"You have talent, and I'm in trouble. Just give me two hours."

"I can't help you," I said. "I have other things to do."

"I know you by now. I know you've built in extra time for yourself. Probably finished just about everything. At this point, you just have to babysit everyone else, right?"

I shrugged. "Mostly. I need to be with the bride when she's getting ready so I can deal with any crises that come up. And I have to put out the wedding favors."

"That'll take, what, fifteen minutes? Come on, Millie. Two hours."

I looked at the sand nervously. "I'm not that good, and I've never sculpted sand before."

"It's easy. This quarry sand is like butter."

"What if I screw it up?"

He smiled. "It's sand. I can fix just about anything. But

you won't screw it up. And I'll put you on the castle. It's straightforward, and I have sketches and a 3D model you can copy. I mean, even Ralph can make a goddamned sand castle."

One corner of my mouth went up. "Thanks," I said drily.

Bennett laughed. "You'll do it. You want to. I know you do. You're an artist, Millie. Be an artist right now."

I looked at him helplessly. I wasn't sure I could ever tell him no. "OK. Two hours. That's it."

"That's enough." He grinned and hugged me. "OK, here's the plan."

I wasn't as fast as Bennett, but over the next two hours and change, in a borrowed T-shirt, my leggings and bare feet, I helped the sand castle and the giant book page around it emerge from the lumps of sand he'd already carved out of the mountain.

When I wasn't bugging him with questions, I sneaked peeks at his work. Piece by piece, he removed the bottom layer of wooden forms so he could create the book that the sand castle and prince and princess were popping out of. He carved amazing detail into the sand couple's bodies and clothes and hair. Soon the book had pages, and words in medieval script on the open page read "Once upon a time . . . "

He showed me how to use a trowel, palette knives, spoons and brushes to get the look I wanted. A straw — he wore a sturdy one on a cord around his neck — allowed us to blow away the particles left in lines and crevices, giving the sculpture a cleaner look.

And I loved it. Sand was easy, easier than clay, as long as I kept it wet and didn't try to get cute with angles and arches. One turret of my castle collapsed as I was trying to carve a window, but Bennett showed me how to build up small parts with wet sand to make a repair.

"Fun, right?" he asked, watching me work as my time neared its end.

I looked up at him, smiling. "It really is. I can see why you love it. Though I have a lot more to learn about technique if I ever want to make anything like that." I nodded at the prince and princess, at their beautiful, rapturous faces and the sense of motion and emotion they had as they rose from the storybook and reached for each other.

"Aw, it ain't nothin'." Bennett reached down and smoothed a rough edge with one finger. "Thanks for your help. I feel good about this now. I have a fair amount left, but it's doable. Finish my couple, wrap up any details you didn't get to, add adornments to the book, carve around it with some fantasy elements, flowers and jewels — "

"Jewels!"

"Diamonds and such. I was listening to you." He smiled. "And then I have to rake what's left around the foundation in the sandbox and make sure everything's super clean around it."

I stood and stretched. "I feel good about it now, too. I love it." *And maybe I love you. When I don't want to kill you.*

We were looking at each other in a kind of awkward emotional haze full of unspoken thoughts when the loading doors opened. Ez walked through, followed by her bandmates carrying boxes and instruments and speakers.

"Millie!" she called as she spotted me.

"Excuse me," I said to Bennett. Sill sans shoes, I padded over to Ez.

"Branching out?" she asked, pushing back her bangs and taking in my sandy appearance. The palette knife was still in my hand.

"Just a little last-minute help. You're here to set up?"

"Thought we should get it done early. Over there, right?"

I nodded. "Yes, that's the stage."

"Believe me, I needed to ask. You never know where people are going to put the band these days. We're doing an electric piano tonight, unless you're hiding a baby grand around here somewhere?"

"Ah, no. They weren't amenable to bringing down the one in the piano lounge."

"That'll be my retirement job," Ez said wistfully. "Playing piano for a bunch of drunk rich people. Hey, Robby!" she screamed to her guitarist. "Over there! Don't forget the lights!"

The long-haired guy hauling two guitars waved her off and started yelling at the other guys.

"Thanks, Ez," I said. "This is going to mean a lot to Alex and Sloane."

"My pleasure. We were coming anyway, and I'd rather play than dance to the fucking 'Electric Slide.' "

I laughed. "Sounds good to me. I'll stop in later this afternoon. Let me know if you need anything."

I returned to Bennett and handed him his knife. "I'll see you later."

"Count on it," he said. "If I miss you at the apartment, I'll meet you here."

"Perfect. It's going to be good."

He smiled. "It's going to be great. Now get out of here!"

The Trifles staff was just starting to lay out the white tablecloths. Place settings would follow. The florist had to add centerpieces. The favors would have to wait until later. I put on my boots and went to the restroom to change back into my tunic top and brush the sand out of my hair. I checked with the venue to make sure they set up the bar for Neil, and I went out to my car to answer messages and make a last round of phone calls.

The people with the ceremonial arch, red carpet and folding chairs arrived as I finished up my call with Cali. I told them where to set up on the beach, checked the blue sky one more time, gave it a thumbs-up, and left to grab a taco before heading over to Alex and Sloane's condo to play lady's maid to the bride.

"It's finally happening," Penelope said to me as the golden hour cast its magical spell on Bohemia Beach. "I can't wait to see the dress in this light."

She'd been with me making sure the dress was perfect before the ceremony. We stood out on the beach, at the back of the mostly seated crowd, which included her boyfriend, Jace, and all of our friends.

Robby, the Emeralds' guitarist, played "I'll Be Home for Christmas" on acoustic guitar up near the arch. Alex stood there, positively dashing in a black tuxedo with a red bow tie, waiting for the bride to walk up the makeshift aisle. The red carpet and sand were scattered with red rose petals. Next to him was the old preacher who'd married his late parents — very old, apparently, and a little deaf. He shouted in normal conversation, but that skill should come in handy this afternoon, with the waves crashing in the background.

The stage was set. Everyone was here. Everyone except Bennett.

I looked toward Trifles again and then the parking lot. One of my streams of thought was oddly calm, sure of the wedding's success, sure I could deal with any issue that might arise. I was ready. But another was wholly occupied by Bennett. He'd finished the sculpture in ample time, as I saw when I'd come back to the ballroom to distribute the favors. It looked spectacular. Two spotlights brought out its dramatic lines and shadows, and the florist had surrounded it with flowers and small Christmas trees lit with white lights. Tears had actually come to Sloane's eyes when she saw it, and I knew I'd made the right choice. But by then, Bennett had gone, and I had missed him at the apartment — if he'd been there at all.

Would he come back?

Robby switched to a different song.

"What is that?" Penelope whispered.

" 'A Winter Romance,' " I replied. Obscure, but that's what the couple wanted.

Those in the know stood, and the rest followed, looking expectantly back toward Trifles. Sloane stepped out of the building on the arm of her father, backlit by a glorious sunset. I'd never met her parents before today, but coming from Ohio, they seemed quite taken with Bohemia Beach. They'd vacationed here a long time ago, and Sloane confided that they were much warmer about Alex once they saw his lavish condo.

As Penelope hinted, Sloane's dress was spectacular. The sinking sun's gilded rays made every crystal on her pale green gown glitter with fire. Sloane was flushed and beaming and adorable, her hair up and threaded with tiny red roses and white orchids, her bouquet lush with big red roses, white orchids, small seashells and tasteful garlands of tiny crystals in red and green.

I glanced back at Alex. I'd always thought him a cool customer. Now he seemed overcome, his face alight with love, his eyes shining at his approaching bride.

Tears came to my own eyes as I watched the short ceremony proceed. The fairy-tale sand sculpture seemed appropriate just then. I knew every relationship had its issues, and Sloane had hinted as much about their courtship, but at this moment, I really believed in happily ever after. At least for some people.

There was a collective gasp partway through the ceremony as a nearly full moon slipped above the horizon behind the couple. I'd taken into account the sunset, but even I was surprised by the moon. The couple gazed at it, then exchanged a knowing glance. It was an incredibly romantic moment.

Finally, it was official, and the crowd cheered as the couple kissed and retreated down the aisle, greeting people as they went. With twilight nigh upon us, the guys lit tiki torches along Trifles' deck. They also ignited the fire bowl there, which was surrounded by stools and comfy chairs, ready for the guests to make s'mores.

"A few formal photos while we have a little light!" Cali called out to the couple.

While she and Wyatt were occupied with getting their shots and the rest of the crowd headed inside for cocktails, I took a moment for myself and walked toward the water, away from the fracas. Outside of the wedding party, the beach was quiet. Even the waves seemed muted in the coolness of dusk. The tide was coming in. A few fluffed-up terns squatted just out of the water's reach in the cool breeze, and I rubbed my arms, chilled despite the long sleeves and long hem of my clingy green velvet dress.

A flash of something white in the water caught my eye, and I stepped forward. There it was again, rolling in the waves. A shell! I didn't want to ruin my shoes, but . . .

"Got it!" He flashed by me, splashing into the waves, grabbing it.

Bennett. In that jacket he'd worn to the party and black pants and a dark blue shirt that matched his indigo eyes.

He carried the seashell to me and pressed the cold, dripping thing into my hands. "Lightning whelk. A nice one." He ran his fingers around the spiral and down the stripes on the shell, stroking my fingers, closing his hands around mine. Then he leaned in and kissed me.

"Thanks," I said after he'd released me. "I thought maybe you weren't coming."

"I got here just when the moon came up. Saw a few

minutes of the ceremony from way back near the building. Didn't want to disrupt anything. Then I checked on the sculpture to make sure Ralph hadn't done anything to it. He gave me dirty looks, but he was so busy with his crew, he didn't have time to do anything else. I don't think he's very happy I'm not dead."

I laughed. "I'm happy both of us aren't dead. Shall we walk back?"

"Ass-bolutely." He took one hand while I carried the shell in the other.

I glanced down. "Oh, no. Your shoes are soaked."

"I have sandals in the van. No one will expect more from the sand sculptor."

"That's right — they don't even know who you are! I have to introduce you to everyone. Sloane loves the sculpture. *Loves* it."

"I live to please."

"I am very pleased with you right now."

"In spite of everything?" Bennett asked, looking down at me.

"Or maybe because of it." I smiled. "You're trouble, do you know that?"

"Always. It's my burden to bear."

I waited until he'd changed into his sandals, and then we entered the ballroom. Inside, fairy lights, abundant flowers, garlands, glowing Christmas trees and mistletoe made it festive. Over the crowd's chatter, Christmas music wafted from the speakers; the band wouldn't play until after dinner. The photographers were getting a few more shots in front of the sand sculpture, to my delight.

"Pose like the prince and princess," Cali told Alex and Sloane, and they obliged, reaching toward each other with goofy smiles on their faces as onlookers laughed.

I introduced Bennett to the couple. To my friends. To anyone who would listen, so they would know he'd made the sculpture. And then I left him chatting with tiki carver Spence Rowan about technique — and left my shell in my bag at our gorgeous table — while I checked to make sure everything else was running smoothly.

I caught up with Cindy by the cake. It was dazzling, much more so than the ice sculpture, which was at the center of the food table, lit by two small spotlights. At least the nipples were more tame than they'd been this morning.

The cake's red, green and clear sugar jewels and snowflakes glimmered in the lights of the ballroom. Garlands of jewels and pearls adorned the four tiers, along with sugar roses in red and shells in white.

"Thanks for making this possible," I told Cindy, "and for keeping everyone sane."

"Oh, he's still insane," she said, nodding at Rafe, who was berating one of his staff by the kitchen door. "But he's a pretty good caterer."

When he's not trying to kill his clients. "I'll never work with him again," I said, "but the food looks great. I hope I get to work with you, though."

"You will. I'm going to start my own business. Plans are already in the works."

"Excellent." I shook her hand. "Catch you later."

The rest of the night was a whirl. Excellent food, killer

cocktails from Neil and the Bohemia Bartenders, funny toasts, dancing and sometimes just rocking to Ez and the Emeralds. Gary filled in on drums as the reception neared its end and the band slowed the pace for a final song.

As Ez's tender rendition of "Have Yourself a Merry Little Christmas" captivated the room, the dance floor filled with good friends. Alex and Sloane were radiant, drunk on each other. Cali and Wyatt put down their cameras and danced, nose to nose in a private conversation. Penelope and Jace looked like movie stars; to be fair, he *was* a movie star. Thea giggled as Duncan grinned, his kilt — a delightful surprise, the women had agreed — flapping as he twirled her.

Bennett found me watching the couples and held out his hand. We joined the others on the dance floor, holding each other close under the sparkle of spinning lights, and beneath my calm exterior, I started to lose it. The job was over. Swaying to the music, looking into Bennett's eyes, I knew I didn't want us to be over, too.

"What are you thinking?" he whispered as we danced.

I just shook my head, not trusting myself to talk, and pulled him closer.

Finally, it was all over — the couple had left for their exotic Galapagos Islands honeymoon trip (via one night in the honeymoon suite of a nearby hotel), everyone pitched in to clean up the stuff the professionals couldn't handle, and I'd distributed checks to the vendors.

The last of these was Neil.

"Thanks," he said from behind the bar. "I want to talk to you. Pull up a barstool."

My mouth quirked. "There are no stools."

"We'll find chairs, then." He dropped one sugar cube each into two rocks glasses, added bitters, muddled them, splashed in club soda.

"Hey, your mustache is different!"

Neil stroked his close-trimmed mustache, now accompanied by a similarly short beard. "Penelope got to me, and then the rest of the women. They told me the handlebar mustache is over. I told them it was part of my identity. And then they said I'd be more hot without it. I hate to say that argument swayed me, but I thought I'd give it a try."

"It's working for you." He really did look handsome. Instead of focusing on the mustache, I admired his face, with its prominent cheekbones and pale gray eyes.

"This is a nice one," Neil said, holding up a bottle of bourbon and measuring out two ounces for each glass. He garnished the cocktails with orange slices and nodded at his fellow bartenders, who were busy packing up gear. "Since they're cleaning up, I'm letting myself have an Old-Fashioned. And you're going to join me."

"Why does it seem like everybody wants me to drink these days?"

"All the kids are doing it," he joked, leading me to a couple of chairs by an empty table. We sat. "I want to hire you."

"What? I'm not a bartender."

"Not as a bartender. Bohemia Bartenders is taking off. I have a cocktail book coming out, and it's getting me — us — gigs at big events."

"That's awesome!" I sipped the drink. Delicious. No wonder this was Cali's favorite.

"I'm excited. We'll be traveling a lot. There will be logistics involved that I'm too busy to deal with, especially since I have The Junction Box to run, too. I need a planner. It's not a full-time job yet, but I can keep you on a retainer, if you're up for it."

We chatted about the job a little more over the drinks, and he agreed to let me think about it.

I had a lot to think about.

I met up with Bennett as the room was nearly broken down, and we headed to the parking lot. That big moon was almost overhead now, casting the world in its cool white glow. A chilly breeze ruffled Bennett's hair.

"Trifles says they want to keep the sculpture up through New Year's," he said. "They sent a photo of it to the clients who have events there over the next week, and not only do they love it, but Trifles wants to have it for their New Year's Eve party."

"That's great!"

"Of course, I told them that it was a custom sculpture just for the wedding and I was contracted to clean it up tomorrow. They said they'd help me with the cleanup after New Year's if I let them keep it."

"You've got a silver tongue, don't you?"

"You would know," Bennett said.

I chuckled and lightly smacked his chest. "I want to make sure the happy couple are OK with having their wedding sculpture show up in other people's pictures."

"Actually, it was Alex who suggested I talk to the venue

about keeping it up for a while. He thought it was sad to tear it down after just one day."

"Wow. You're way ahead of me." I looked up at the moon and rocked on my low heels. "So I guess this is it."

"What do you mean?"

I wasn't ready to tell him what I really meant. "The wedding's over. I have to figure out what I'm going to do when I grow up."

"Oh, yeah. I have some ideas about that. But let's talk about them at your place. It's getting cold out here for a Florida boy."

"Wimp!"

"Am not!" He chased me to my car. When he caught me, he kissed me, and I got lost for a minute in his sweet heat as the chilly breeze swirled around us.

When he released me, a funny feeling prickled my spine. Something was odd.

I knew that feeling. It was the same one I had when Bennett put that birthday banner on Rafe's shop.

I glanced up at Bennett, who wore a coy expression, and then I looked around. At the other end of the dark parking lot, there was a strange van. An unusually tall van. An unusually tall Broussard's van with something wrong with the wheels.

"What is that?" I asked.

Bennett looked at me with a wide-eyed expression. "You mean Ralph's van?"

"Oh, no."

"You said I couldn't mess with him *before* the wedding."

I walked over to the big panel van and looked more closely at the wheels. "How did you do that?"

The van and its tires were suspended in midair. The frame of the van between the wheels rested on stacks of cinder blocks that lifted it up so high, the tires didn't touch the ground. The whole vehicle was elevated, poised precariously in a completely undrivable position.

"The surfer dudes were willing to help me do one more job for cash. They're out having a really nice Christmas Eve right now."

I nodded, amazed. I looked up at Bennett. "Well done."

"What?" Bennett laughed in surprise.

"He deserves it after what he tried to do to us. He's lucky we didn't call the cops. But after Alex and Sloane are done with their honeymoon, I'm going to make sure they know exactly what he did."

Bennett nodded. "That's only fair. I look forward to Alex ruining that prick."

"He should be able to get the food for his fundraiser out of Rafe first."

Bennett followed me back to my car.

"Wait a minute," I said. "Where's your van?"

"It still wouldn't start. Took an Uber. It's better. Now I can ride home with you."

"Oh." I smiled. "That's nice. Good thing I only had one drink."

IT GOT warm pretty fast at my apartment. Despite the fact

that both of us were beat, we drank champagne and snuggled and kissed for a while on the couch by the light of the Christmas tree, lulled by the relaxing piano of Vince Guaraldi's *A Charlie Brown Christmas* soundtrack. Soon we were practically falling asleep in each other's arms, and by mutual agreement, we stumbled to the bedroom, stripped and slept hard.

I awakened in the morning to the sound of faraway church bells.

"Is that playing 'It Came Upon the Midnight Clear'?" Bennett murmured into his pillow.

"I think so," I said, snuggling up to him.

He shifted me, spooned me, caressing my behind, my legs. It was really nice waking up naked with a naked man. With Bennett.

"I think you're the best present I ever got on Christmas morning," I said softly, almost hoping he didn't hear me.

"Is that right?" he whispered into my ear. "Are you drunk?"

"Very sober. I'm glad you're here, Bennett."

"So am I, darling Milia." He kissed my neck, my shoulders. His hand slipped between my legs from behind, stroking me there, finding me more than ready for him.

"Are you — protected?" he asked. "If not, I can get — "

"I'm good," I said. I'd recently gone on the pill. Very recently, but for long enough that I knew it was effective.

"So am I," he murmured. "I've wanted to do this for so long. Be bare inside you."

I groaned as he eased his cock between my legs, into my slippery cleft, stretching me, already taking me close to the boiling point. He stayed there for a moment, his breaths coming short.

"More," I said.

"Yes." He pulled out, thrust deeper. "Yes, Millie." Again. "Yes, sweet Milia. *Yes.*"

Slow and hard and tight, hot and deep and achingly good. That was Bennett driving inside me as we lay sideways on the bed, my back to his front, my soft body enfolded in his hard one. He held me close, one arm under my breasts, the other lower, reaching around my front to cup my mound. He flicked and teased my bud, doubling my rapture; pinched it, and then I was gone, a snowflake tossed by the wind, soaring, spinning into the dazzling light.

I cried out, clenching around him. I felt him detonate inside me, raw and powerful. I shattered again as he convulsed, lost in the visceral pleasure of feeling him pulsing there.

Finally, he slumped against me, kissing my shoulders, my neck. After a moment, he slid out and turned me to him, devouring my mouth with his.

He paused with a sigh. "Will you plan my life for me, Millie?"

"What?" I let out a bubble of surprised laughter.

"I'm serious. I want you there with me, every minute, every day. If you can't be there, I want to know you're marking the days off on your calendar until I come home."

"Bennett?"

He gave me a small, wry smile. "Are you confused?"

"Maybe. Am I dreaming?"

"How can we make this work? You and me. Forever."

"Really?" I kissed him. "Really?"

"What do you think I've been doing, hanging around Bohemia Beach for the past month? I want you, and not just like this. Though this is pretty good."

"Yes, it is." I kissed him again. "I want this, too. You. Everything."

"Everything." He laughed. "OK, we can try everything."

"I think I like being a planner."

"A wedding planner?"

"That, and more. I talked to Neil last night. His bartender business is taking off. He has events on the calendar, and he needs a coordinator. Someone like me who can schedule and book their trips, manage supplies, set things up. I'm good at that."

"Yes, you are," Bennett said. "I want you to do the same thing for me."

"You do?" I guess he saw the doubt in my eyes.

"Not just that. I want you, not just your organizational skills."

"That's good."

"Here, wait a minute." He eased out of bed, went to the living room and came back with a present, a box wrapped in silver paper with a pretty green ribbon. "This is for you," he said, handing it to me and slipping back under the covers.

"This is a first for me. Opening presents naked in bed on Christmas morning."

"As long as it's not full of glitter, I don't see a problem." He grinned.

"I wouldn't put it past you." I tore off the paper and lifted the lid. Nestled in red tissue paper was a small palette knife. I looked up at him, not quite understanding.

"I don't just want you to plan for me. I want you to sculpt with me, too, when you can. Travel with me. You can make your art, have your adventure. Have it with me." His eyes searched mine for reaction, reassurance. "You're my adventure, darling Milia."

Tears pricked my eyes, and I cupped him by the chin and kissed him. "Yes, Bennett. I want to do all the things. The planning. The art. The travel with you." I took a deep breath. "I love you, you know."

"I didn't know, but I hoped. I love you, too. I never thought I'd really love anyone until I met you. I liked you at the diner, angel that you were, but I loved you at the bar, drunk and funny and smart and earnest. And then everything you did to keep me on track" — he kissed my neck — "and every kiss that made me wild" — he licked my sensitive earlobe — "made me love you more."

He grabbed the palette knife and tossed it on the nightstand before enveloping me in his arms, crushing his mouth against mine.

Finally, we took a breath, and I held him close, overwhelmed at all the possibilities, my life blown wide open.

"So where's my present?" he teased.

I chuckled, rolling back to give us some air. It's funny how warm it got with someone like Bennett.

"I got you a present," I said, "but it was more out of hope than anything. I didn't think I could give it to you, so I didn't even wrap it."

"I don't mind."

"OK, wait here." I slipped out of bed, bent over and rummaged in my closet for the gift. "Close your eyes."

"But I'm so enjoying the view of your ass."

"Bennett! Eyes closed." I found it.

"OK. They're closed."

I turned around, taking the braided leather bracelet out of the box. "Hold out your arm."

He did as I asked, and I wrapped the leather around his wrist.

"Is this some kind of kinky thing, because, oh my God, I think I'm going to pop my cap."

I giggled as I fastened it. "No. We can negotiate that later."

He grinned, his eyes still closed. "You make me so crazy."

"I know." I slipped under the covers next to him. "Open your eyes."

Oh, those eyes. With a curious expression, Bennett touched the brown leather braid, wound three times around his wrist, and turned it until he saw the silver anchor caught by the loop that fastened it in place.

He smiled. "Millie! Aw, you're my anchor."

"Better than the ol' ball and chain."

He chuckled and looked up at me. "It's perfect. You're perfect."

"No, I'm not, but I'm happy. Really happy. You are the present I didn't even know I wanted, not until I met you. Merry Christmas."

"Merry Kissmas." His kiss was even more incendiary

this time, and I resisted the urge to throw off the covers to cool down.

"Are we ever going to get out of bed?" I asked.

"Maybe for New Year's?"

I tangled my feet with his. "We might have to get out of bed for Christmas dinner. My parents will send a search party if I don't show up. Are you up for it? They're Italian. You won't have to eat for weeks afterward."

"Count me in. I'm in for the long haul." Bennett's lips found mine again. "Besides, that's hours away. I can think of a few things to do until then."

"Show me," I whispered.

The bells rang a carol of joy and promise as he pulled me under the covers.

AFTERWORD

Thanks for reading! Sign up for my newsletter to get fun original content, giveaways, news and cocktail recipes, and I'll send you a free story. I also have a Facebook group where readers can hang out and chat about books and life — please join us in Lucy's Lounge.

MORE ONLINE:

LucyLakestone.com

Facebook.com/LucyLakestone

Twitter.com/LucyLakestone

Bookbub.com/authors/lucy-lakestone

Pinterest.com/lucylakestone/

Amazon

Goodreads

YouTube

ABOUT THE AUTHOR

Lucy Lakestone is an award-winning author who lives on Florida's east central coast, among the towns that serve as an inspiration for the hot romances of her Bohemia Beach Series, including *Bohemia Beach, Bohemia Light, Bohemia Blues* (winner of the Golden Quill), *Bohemia Heat, Bohemia Nights* and *Bohemia Bells*. She's been a journalist, photographer, editor and video producer but prefers living in her imagination, where the moon is full and the cocktails are divine. She is also the author of a novel of romantic suspense, *Desire on Deadline*.

ACKNOWLEDGMENTS

THE BOHEMIA BEACH SERIES reaches its conclusion — or a natural pause — with *Bohemia Bells*. The entire series takes place in just over a year. Each novel begins at the event where the last one left off, but from the point of view of a different heroine. Most of the stories adhere strictly to a calendar from one year, so the moon phases, tides and sunrises are authentic. Thus it was a wonderful surprise to look up what the moon was doing on Christmas Eve in my chosen year and see that it was nearly full and rising just as Alex and Sloane were having their ceremony on the beach. I was as stunned as Millie and just as thrilled, as the moon always seems to be looking over my characters.

I'm deeply grateful to Jill Harris and Thomas Koet of Sandsational Sand Sculpting for their friendship and insights into what goes into making one of their fantastic works of art.

I owe huge thanks to my editor, Holly Martin, for her investment in the series and her encouragement. The

Rocket Girls have been wonderful, too, during stolen writing sessions at the coffee shop, especially Alethea Kontis and Naomi Bellina.

Thanks to the members of Lucy's Lounge on Facebook for your feedback on the cover and more. I wish I could mix you all an Old-Fashioned! I greatly appreciate the readers who have plunged into the series, left nice reviews and given me hope that it's OK sometimes to stray from the obvious path when it comes to writing.

Always ready with a cocktail, Mr. Lakestone has somehow survived my mountains of books and paper and eccentric writing schedule. I couldn't do this without him.

Although I see *Bohemia Bells* as the conclusion to the Bohemia Beach Series, I won't rule out revisiting it again sometime in the future. And a spinoff series of romantic mysteries is coming soon starring the Bohemia Bartenders. Get ready to be shaken *and* stirred.

BOOKS BY LUCY LAKESTONE

The **BOHEMIA BEACH** Series

Award-winning romance by Lucy Lakestone

In a beautiful small city on Florida's east coast, artists struggle to make their way. Where creative minds meet and restless hearts yearn, where emotion and ambition vie with lust and dark secrets, romance is impossible to resist. Welcome to the seductive tropical escape they call home – Bohemia Beach.

These steamy contemporary romances are the perfect escape for anyone who loves a love story with lots of heat and a shot of laughter. Though the books have a common setting and characters, each can be read as a standalone novel.

BOHEMIA BEACH

BOHEMIA LIGHT

BOHEMIA BLUES

BOHEMIA HEAT

BOHEMIA NIGHTS

BOHEMIA BELLS

and don't miss

DESIRE ON DEADLINE